# THE RANGE WAR OF '82

# THE RANGE WAR OF '82

# ETHAN J. WOLFE

**FIVE STAR**

*A part of Gale, Cengage Learning*

GALE
CENGAGE Learning®

Farmington Hills, Mich • San Francisco • New York • Waterville, Maine
Meriden, Conn • Mason, Ohio • Chicago

## GALE
### CENGAGE Learning·

LIBRARY OF CONGRESS CATALOGING-IN-PUBLICATION DATA

Wolfe, Ethan J.
   The range war of '82 / by Ethan J. Wolfe. — First edition.
      pages ; cm
      ISBN 978-1-4328-3072-4 (hardcover) — ISBN 1-4328-3072-4 (hardcover)
   1. Farmers—Wyoming—Fiction. 2. Ranchers—Wyoming—Fiction. 3. Cattle trade—Wyoming—Fiction. 4. Wyoming—History—19th century—Fiction. I. Title.
PS3612.A5433R36 2015
813'.6—dc23                                              2015008340

Find us on Facebook– https://www.facebook.com/FiveStarCengage
Visit our website– http://www.gale.cengage.com/fivestar/
Contact Five Star™ Publishing at FiveStar@cengage.com

Printed in Mexico
3 4 5 6 7 8 20 19 18 17 16

# THE RANGE WAR OF '82

# 1930

I was but a boy of eight years old in the spring of 1882, the year of the great range war that changed so many lives and the valley itself. Wyoming wasn't yet a state and land was plentiful, and three years earlier my father moved his family west from Wisconsin to start a new life for us. He sold the family farm he inherited from his father, one of two his father owned in Wisconsin, and used the money to buy one hundred and sixty acres of fertile land in the vast Wyoming valley.

So did many other families, and that didn't sit well with the cattle ranchers as they needed as much open range as possible to breed their herds. Cattle require a great deal of land and a healthy supply of water for a herd and a rancher to prosper and grow.

Farmers require the same, plentiful land and water.

For many years afterward I often reflected back upon those wild days of the old west and dreamed of the simplicity and of the danger. I had no knowledge of the telephone or electric lightbulb, the phonograph player and many other things that had sprung up back east. The town barber oftentimes doubled for a doctor and often rye whiskey served as the only medicine available. My education consisted of what my mother was able to teach me and from what I observed on my own.

She taught me well. I was able to read and write and do the multiplication table and put those skills to good use when I started a journal.

7

In 1890, at the state fair, I discovered photography and fell in love with it. In 1900 I went to work for the newspaper in Casper as a photographer and spent five happy years documenting the quickly changing wild west.

The year was 1905 when I traveled east to New Jersey to study the Edison Motion Picture Camera and my life changed forever. Edison made motion pictures, and for a nickel you could view them at a nickelodeon.

I directed my first silent film, a western, in 1911. It ran thirty-five minutes. Between 1911 and 1929, I directed forty-three silent films, mostly westerns, all one hour in length. The good guys wore white hats and always won. You may remember my name from reading film credits, Seth Johansen.

So in 1930, not long after the stock market crash of 1929, I was as surprised as anybody when the biggest Hollywood studio hired me to direct a two-hour western based upon a script I wrote and submitted for approval. It was budgeted at one million dollars, a vast amount of money, and it was to be the first western with sound. No reading the actors' words on screen, but hearing their actual voices as they spoke.

The crew was large, for the film was large and expensive. I hired the best costume designers available. I convinced the studio to let me film on location in Wyoming for the realism, rather than on a back lot, and they agreed. My younger brother Jesse served as my assistant as he had many times before, and I asked him to locate an old cowboy I once knew to serve as technical advisor on the film.

I wanted to make the most realistic western to date, and not just to please audiences and the studio bosses. I felt the story just needed to be told as it was a part of the historic flavor of the old west itself.

So on a spring morning, while I was scouting locations in Wyoming, my brother sent a telegram that he'd located the old cowboy and they would be arriving by train in the morning. They would meet us at our hotel.

And this is that story.

The story of the Great Range War of 1882.

And of the gunfighter who saved my life.

I wrote it partly from memory and a great deal of it from what my mother told me much later in her life.

Here is a bit of that story as best as I can write it.

# ONE

Seth Johansen came out of the barn holding the large round pan he used to feed the chickens. It was heavy, loaded with feed. The chickens, of which there were many, flocked around him as he carried the pan to their coop.

The chickens pecked and squawked as he tossed the feed around and when the pan was empty, he returned it to the barn and got ready for his next chore. At four thirty in the morning, it wasn't quite sunup yet, but the lightening sky was so beautiful a sight, so vast and wide, that he had to pause to look at it.

Standing in the open barn door, Seth stared at the horizon and daydreamed. Across the way, the shutter on the kitchen window snapped open and Seth's father, James Johansen, poked his head out.

"Seth, them chickens ain't going to gather up their own eggs, and the cow ain't going to milk herself," James said. "If you want breakfast I suggest you quit watching the sky and get to it. The sky can wait, the cow can't."

Seth snapped from his funk. "Yes, Pa."

He went to the rear of the chicken coop and used his mother's straw basket to gather up the eggs laid by the hens overnight. Eleven large white eggs and two smaller brown ones.

Seth wasn't sure why sometimes the chickens laid brown eggs. He asked everybody, but no one could tell him why. His mother said there was no difference between the two, like with people when he asked her about the black family that made the trip west with the others.

She told him that what color a person's skin is has nothing to do with what kind of person he or she is. She taught him about the Civil War and the hardships the slaves had to endure for hundreds of years. He didn't quite understand it all, and the confusion of it grew when he met the Jones family on the trip west.

Mal Jones had been born a slave in 1849, as had his wife Keri. They picked cotton on something called a plantation in the state of Georgia. They had a son named Cal, who was about Seth's age. They played together many times and Seth didn't see what the big deal was over the color of their skin.

After he carried the basket of eggs to the open kitchen window, Seth returned to the barn to milk the cow. The cow had a separate stall in the barn away from Pa's two massive plow horses.

Seth wasn't allowed to go near the horses. Pa told him so massive a beast with so little intelligence could accidently kick you without even knowing it, although the only thing Seth ever saw them do was stand there and occasionally brush flies with their tails.

He set the bucket and stool in place, warmed his hands by blowing on them, and got to milking the cow. He wanted to name her, but Pa said it was a foolish idea to name an animal you might one day have to eat in hard times.

It didn't take long to empty the udders. Inside of twenty minutes the gallon bucket was full of fresh milk and slowly rising cream. Seth covered the bucket and carefully carried it into the house.

The kitchen was the biggest room in the house and was dominated by a large stone fireplace in front of the table and chairs. Pa had built a long baking counter for Ma beside the front loaded oven, and when she was cooking or baking it gave off enough heat to warm the entire house in the fall months. Beside the counter Pa had installed a hand pump for fresh water. Another pump and well was outside beside the small corral.

Pa was at the table waiting for breakfast. Ma was at the stove preparing it.

"About time," Pa said. "Did you fill the bowl beside the door?"

"Not yet, Pa," Seth said.

Seth carried the bucket to Ma and set it down. He lifted the lid and used a ladle to scoop out some of the milk and then carried it back outside and filled the wood bowl beside the door. Sometime during the day the cat would show up from where he'd been sleeping and drink the milk. He was a big stray who wandered in one day, and Pa said it was a good idea to leave him food so he'd hang around and catch mice and scare off a fox that had eyes on the chickens.

Every once in a while, when he was doing schoolwork with Ma at the table, the cat would jump through the open window and rub his legs. The cat'd have some new battle wound or scar from a fight with whatever animal that dared to challenge him.

"Seth?" Ma called. "Come wash your hands and have breakfast."

Seth returned to the kitchen and cranked the pump at the sink. Cold water flowed. He used the bar of soap Ma made from fat and scented oils and scrubbed his hands clean, then cranked the pump again to rinse them.

About to wipe his hands on his shirt, Ma said, "Use the towel, Seth."

He used the towel and took his place beside his pa.

Ma served scrambled eggs, strips of bacon, toasted bread from the loaf she had baked yesterday with butter she had churned yesterday, a glass of milk for Seth and coffee for Pa.

13

"Bacon, Ma?" Seth said. "It ain't Sunday, is it?"

"Isn't Sunday," Ma said. "We do not use the word ain't, remember?"

"Pa says ain't all the time," Seth said.

"When you're a full-grown man with your own family you can speak however you want to," Ma said. "In the meantime you will do as I say. Now eat."

"Yes, Ma," Seth said.

He looked at Pa, who winked at him. They waited for Ma to say grace and then they ate breakfast.

After breakfast Seth helped Ma clear the table and put the dishes and pans in the sink and cranked the pump to fill the basin and let them soak.

"I'll be in the north field today," Pa said. "Seth, you bring me my lunch."

"Yes, Pa."

"And mind your schooling."

"Yes, Pa."

After Pa left, Seth helped Ma skim the cream off the milk and poured it into the churner. Ma would spend the next hour churning the cream into butter for tomorrow.

"Take the milk to the icehouse," Ma said.

"Yes, Ma," Seth said.

He covered the milk bucket and carried it from the house to the small icehouse Pa built the first summer they moved from the Great Woods to Wyoming. Almost everybody in the Wisconsin woods had an icehouse to store blocks of ice in for summer use. Constructed of wood walls lined with many layers of straw and mud, ice was cut out of frozen rivers and lakes, carried to the house and wrapped in burlap and then stacked. The ice would last all summer, and no matter how hot it got in June, July and August, the icehouse was always cold.

Seth set the milk bucket beside the blocks of ice. Pa had built shelves against the back wall and Ma used them to store butter and other perishables. Under the shelves rested a fifty-pound bag of potatoes and another of carrots. In the cold, each would last for months.

Seth closed and locked the icehouse door with the plank of wood that dropped into the slots Pa had attached into the walls on each side of the door.

Ma was churning the cream when Seth returned to the house.

"Seth, go finish your chores. When I'm done here, we'll do your schoolwork until it's time to take your father his lunch," Ma said.

"Yes, Ma," Seth said.

"And try not to play with that cat, if he's around," Ma said. "We don't want him to become friendly or he'll get fat and lazy."

"Yes, Ma," Seth said and went outside to finish his chores.

# TWO

James Johansen, at thirty-four years of age, was a tall man for the day. At five foot, nine inches tall, he stood three inches taller than the average man. He had wide shoulders and thick, powerful wrists and forearms developed from a lifetime of hard work in the fields.

His eyes were blue, but his hair was dark. That was unusual, for almost everyone in his Swedish family was blond or light haired. His parents emigrated from Sweden in 1844, and he was the first in the bloodline to be born in America. His parents chose Wisconsin to settle in for several reasons. They were farmers back home and Wisconsin was good farmland. It also had the same climate as Sweden and they were comfortable with that.

While life could be harsh in their adopted state, it could also be good, and the Johansen farm grew along with most others in the North Woods. The war didn't reach them, and it wasn't unusual to see black folks from the south start a new life among them.

By the time he was nineteen, James was an accomplished farmer and had learned to grow just about anything. His father taught him about land conservation and crop rotation, irrigation and how to spread nutrients into the soil for coming years.

Shortly after his nineteenth birthday, James met Sarah Ingersoll at the Independence Day barbecue, where the entire community gathered to celebrate the day.

16

Sarah was just thirteen at the time, but James knew immediately that she would be his wife in the future. Barely five feet tall, Sarah had dark hair and green eyes that seemed to reflect light and change color in sunlight and darkness.

Protocol dictated he wait until Sarah turned sixteen to begin to woo her. Two years later, a day after she turned eighteen, they were married. They were happy for several years living on the Johansen farm. Seth was born one year after the wedding, crops were good and, while no one grew wealthy, they didn't lack for comfort.

Slowly things began to change as the population swelled around them. Shortly after Seth turned four, James made the decision to move west and start their own farm in a new land.

Wyoming offered such a new start. It was wide open territory with land aplenty. James wired the appropriate banks and developers, and after six months of negotiations and financing, he moved the family west to their new home.

They said their good-byes in the late winter of 1878 and traveled by covered wagon through Minnesota and into South Dakota and finally to the rich, fertile valley in Wyoming.

They arrived intact in early spring. The first spring and summer were spent constructing the house, barn and corral, and they lived off their savings and money sent from the family back in Wisconsin. The one hundred and sixty acres James purchased was already cleared, but had been untouched in years. He spent the following spring getting it ready.

That second spring, James planted forty acres of wheat and forty acres of corn, leaving the remaining eighty acres for the next season. That second spring also saw six additional farms spring up. The year after that brought another eight.

That was the year the trouble started.

After two hours of turning the soil, James gave the horses a breather to cool down a bit. He walked to the wagon and drank from the canteen. Drenched in sweat, James removed his work shirt but kept the long sleeve undershirt on. He would rather sweat than get sunburned.

Off in the distance he could see faint smoke bellowing from the chimney. Sarah probably had bread in the oven and maybe pie made with sweet potatoes. The thought of the pie made his stomach rumble with hunger. Breakfast seemed so long ago and the hard fieldwork whet a man's appetite.

James looked at the placement of the sun in the sky and estimated it would be another two hours before Seth showed up with his lunch.

Taking another sip from the canteen, James wiped his brow and returned to the horses and continued plowing.

To his right was prime land ripe for farming. At least another one hundred and sixty acres. It was owned by the bank in Casper, and as far as James knew hadn't been sold yet. He wanted that land. It would double the size of his farm and production and make life more comfortable for them in the years to come.

The problem was he needed twelve hundred dollars to buy it and all he had in the bank was three hundred. The bank told him they required half to sell him the land on a mortgage.

That was another two years of saving. By then another family was sure to buy it and cultivate the land.

By noon ten acres of the forty had been turned. He spotted Seth with the lunch pail and stopped the horses. He walked to the wagon for grain and fed the horses while Seth continued walking.

Then, together, they sat in the wagon to eat lunch.

Cold pork sandwiches on freshly baked bread, apples and cold milk in a quart canteen.

"What did your ma teach you this morning?" James said.

"Multiplication, addition and the Revolutionary War," Seth said.

"Good subjects," James said.

"Pa, if I'm going to work the farm with you, why do I have to know all that stuff?" Seth asked.

"That *stuff*, as you called it, is important," James said.

"Why?"

"Well, do you know that land over there I'd like to buy?"

Seth nodded.

"The bank says it's one hundred and sixty acres," James said. "And costs twelve hundred dollars. How would you know what one hundred and sixty is if you can't count? And how would you know how much twelve hundred dollars is if you can't add money? Understand?"

"Yes, Pa," Seth said. "I understand that, but what good is it to know all this history stuff?"

"Well, a man should know about his country, about where it came from and where it's going," James said. "That way it becomes part of you, and you become part of it. Understand?"

"I think so."

"Good," James said. "Now finish lunch. I got work to do."

To the left of the wagon about three hundred yards away were rolling hills. Atop those hills Seth spotted three men on horseback. They weren't riding. They were still, as if watching them.

"Pa, there are three men on the hills yonder," Seth said.

"I see them," James said. "They been there for a while now. Parker's men spying on me."

"Why?"

"Why does one man spy on another?" James said. "Because they're nosey about other people's business."

"How come?"

"Never mind," James said. "Some people just are. Now go home and help your ma with the chores. Tell her I'll be along around four thirty."

"Yes, Pa."

"Leave the bucket. I'll bring it back in the wagon."

Seth hopped off the back of the wagon and started the long walk home. Hoping Pa didn't catch him, he glanced over his shoulder at the three men on horseback. They were still motionless, although one of them appeared to be smoking a cigarette now.

James went around to the front seat of the wagon and turned his back to the three men on the hill so they wouldn't see him lift his father's old Navy Colt revolver off the seat and tuck it under his undershirt.

He returned to his plowing, thinking that if the three men rode down looking for trouble, he would at least be able to give them some.

# THREE

Sarah Johansen didn't exactly feel old at the age of twenty-eight; more like worn out and in need of a good long rest. Having been raised on a farm, she knew the hardships as well as the rewards of being a farmer, the sunup-to-sundown, never-ending stream of work, but she wished sometimes that life could be easier.

Sometimes—mostly when she was alone—she missed her family back in Wisconsin, but then Seth would get underfoot and those moments would pass quickly. She thought about asking James if they could return to Wisconsin for a visit, but she knew he wouldn't agree to go and she wouldn't go without him.

Not with the farm finally turning a profit after two years of hard work. And he did work hard. Backbreaking work in the fields all spring, summer and fall. Even during the winter months James always found something to do that needed to be done to keep the farm running smoothly. Repairing the hoes, axes, and other equipment, fixing things in the barn and house and getting things ready for spring.

Their savings were building up in the bank, and James wanted that vacant field adjacent to theirs. He would never agree to spend money to travel east to visit the family. No, she would have to be content with monthly letters filled with news and activities of their family and friends.

Sarah heard Seth open the front door, and she came out of the bedroom where she had been washing the wood floor.

"Pa says he'll be home around four thirty," Seth said.

"I thought about baking a pie for tonight," Sarah said. "While I finish the floors would you get a fire going in the stove?"

"What kind of pie, Ma?"

"If you bring me ten apples from the icehouse I'll tell you," Sarah said.

Seth started for the door, and Sarah said, "And don't forget the fire."


Seth carried the steaming hot apple pie from the oven to the window ledge to set it to cool. Pa would be home in two hours, and by then the center would still be warm and luscious. Thinking about it made his mouth water.

"Seth, grab your books and let's do an hour of schoolwork before you do your afternoon chores," Sarah said.

"Yes, Ma."

Seth fetched his writing book and pencil from his bedroom and sat at the table. Sarah poured two glasses of cold milk and then she opened her teacher's lesson book that she insisted James buy from the catalog in the general store in town.

"How about history?" Sarah suggested.

"Okay, Ma."

For the next hour they studied the Civil War and the Thirteenth Amendment that freed the slaves. Seth wasn't sure why they needed a new law for people to be free. He knew God created all men in his own image, and he doubted God had the idea one man should own another when he set about creating things.

When the hour was up, Sarah said, "Now go do your chores before your father gets home."

"Yes, Ma," Seth said. "Oh, I almost forgot. When I brought Pa his lunch there were three men on horses watching him from the hill."

"Three men?" Sarah said.

"Pa said they was . . ."

"Were."

"Pa said they were Mr. Parker's men," Seth said.

"Did they do anything?"

"They just sat on the hill and watched Pa."

"Very well, go do your chores now."

Seth went to the barn and filled the pan with feed for the chickens. After they were fed, he filled the grain sacks for the horses and then swept out the stalls. The cow was getting restless, so next he set about milking her and carried the bucket into the house for Ma to skim off the cream for the butter. After that he walked the cow into the corral, where she would spend the night eating sweet grass. Pa always said the sweeter the grass, the sweeter the milk.

He was back in the barn pitching a bale of hay when he heard Pa's wagon outside. He dropped the pitchfork and ran outside to greet him.

"Chores all done?" Pa said.

"Almost."

"I smell pie," Pa said.

"Apple," Seth said. "I cored the apples."

"Let's get the horses put away and wash up," Pa said. "I'm starving."

Sarah said grace over the fine supper she prepared of fried chicken, potatoes, carrots, milk for Seth and Sarah, coffee for James.

After Seth and Sarah cleared the table, Sarah served the apple pie.

Seth had another glass of milk and James another cup of coffee.

Sarah picked her spot to bring up the subject. James was always easier to talk to when his stomach was full.

"Seth told me Parker's men were spying on you again," Sarah said.

"They didn't bother me," James said.

"That isn't the point," Sarah said. "People shouldn't spy on people without a very good reason, and we've given them none."

"They weren't on our land, so I had no right to ask them to leave," James said. "And they made no move to trespass or even speak to me, so it seems there's nothing to do about it at the present time."

"I still think you should talk to the sheriff," Sarah said.

"And tell him what? That three men were looking at me?" James said. "Besides, it was Parker who had the sheriff appointed."

"What's appointed?" Seth said.

"It means he was chosen for the job without being elected," Sarah said.

"Like when Pa appoints me a new chore?" Seth said.

James laughed. "That's one way of putting it," he said.

Seth eyed the half still left of the pie. "Can I have another piece, Ma?"

"A small one," Sarah said. "I want to save the rest for breakfast."

"I need to replace the brake on the wagon," James said. "It's rusted out. I was thinking of taking the afternoon off tomorrow and going to town. I'd like to bring Seth with me."

"Can I, Ma?" Seth said with sudden excitement.

"If you finish your chores and schoolwork by the time your father is ready to leave," Sarah said. "And only one penny candy. Understand me?"

"Yes, Ma."

"I believe I'll sit on the porch for a bit and smoke my pipe," James said.

"Help me clear the table and you can join your father," Sarah told Seth.

Seth was always amazed at how beautiful the sky looked just before sunset. The clouds glowed orange and red and the ground appeared almost yellow. The sun, a giant ball of red, slowly sank below the horizon, and the colors in the sky hung on for a bit longer until it all went dark.

"Seth, get ready for bed," Sarah said when night fell.

"Yes, Ma," Seth said and went inside.

James emptied his pipe by banging it against the porch railing and then fed it fresh tobacco. As he struck a match, he looked at Sarah.

Sarah lowered her eyes.

"I don't understand it," James said.

"There is no understanding God's way, James," Sarah said.

"Are you saying God doesn't want us to have a second son?" James said.

"No, I'm not saying that," Sarah said. She knew that James feared two miscarriages in three years might have left her barren. "I'm saying we don't understand why certain things happen. We will just have to keep trying and praying and that's all we can do."

James sucked on his pipe. "I suppose."

Seth came out wearing his nightshirt to say good night. He kissed Sarah on the cheek. "Night, Ma."

"Get your rest, son," James said. "Tomorrow we're going to town."

# FOUR

The town of Brooks was founded in 1849 by a man named Jed Brooks. At the time of its founding, he was its only occupant. He dreamed of creating a trail for cattlemen to drive their herds east to Nebraska for slaughter, and the best way to do that was to create a township.

Indian raids killed him in 1850, and his lone building stood for seven years until another cattleman, a much wealthier man named Monroe Parker, with the same dream, moved his ranch north from Texas and settled in for good. Monroe had a son he named Jefferson after Thomas Jefferson. When Monroe died in 1867, his son assumed the role of cattle baron in the territory.

As Jefferson Parker grew in wealth and land, so did the town. Now, in 1882, Brooks had a swollen population of two hundred thirty citizens, who were almost all in some way tied to the cattle ranches that surrounded the town.

Now forty-nine years old, Parker knew the time was ripe for expansion of the town and his own wealth. He wasn't satisfied with the biggest ranch with the largest herd. He knew the only way for continued growth and prosperity was to convince the railroad to build a connector line to bring cattle directly to Santa Fe for shipping east to Nebraska and Chicago, west to California and south all the way into Texas.

With that accomplishment statehood would follow, and who better to be the first elected governor of the new state than the man behind this driving force?

All that stood between Parker and his dream were the new breed of farmers plaguing the territory. Oh, he knew people had to eat more than beef, but farmers could grow their corn and wheat almost anywhere, so why did they have to pick here, in the heart of cattle country?

The territorial bankers encouraged the farmers to come with mortgage incentives and land tax breaks and such. There wasn't much Parker could do about that at the present time. Statehood with a governor would change all that, and Parker was determined to be that very first governor.

Looking out the front window of the First Bank of Brooks, Parker sipped coffee and watched the street.

"Mr. Parker?" Wilson, the bank president, said from his desk.

Parker turned away from the window.

"I have the information you requested," Wilson said.

Parker walked to the desk and sat in the chair opposite. "And?"

"Four of those vacant fields have been purchased by families back east," Wilson said. "The land adjacent to the Johansen place is vacant at the moment, but Mr. Johansen has made inquiries on it."

"How much for that plot?" Parker said.

"The territory will only sell for the purpose of farming," Wilson said.

"Oh, damn them," Parker said. "What do they know of the territory's own potential? What if I buy it and do nothing with the land?"

"The mortgage becomes null and void," Wilson said.

"The railroad is coming here to talk to me," Parker said. "The telegraph will be here in another year and there's talk of phone lines by nineteen hundred. Do you think those things will happen because farmers grow some wheat?"

"That isn't the point," Wilson said.

"What is the point then, if not progress?"

"The territorial governor doesn't want one group to have dominant power over another," Wilson said. "And you already know that."

Parker set his coffee cup on the desk and stood up. "This territory will never get statehood with thinking like that," he said.

"Maybe so, but that's the way it is right now," Wilson said.

Parker left the bank and walked along the wood sidewalk to the office he built in town. A sign above the office door read *Parker Cattle Ranch. J. Parker Owner.*

Sheriff Smiley was standing around with a couple of Parker's men.

"Boys, I'd like a word with the sheriff in private," Parker said. The men left the office.

Smiley lifted the coffeepot off the woodstove and poured a cup. "I take it things didn't go your way with the bank," he said.

"They're more interested in growing corn and wheat than in statehood," Parker said. "Fools, every last one of them."

Smiley shrugged. "What can you do?" he said.

"Drive them out, that's what I can do," Parker said.

"There's no legal cause for that," Smiley said.

"Now you sound like Wilson," Parker said.

"Wilson is just trying to . . ."

"Don't tell me what he's trying to do," Parker said. "I know what he's trying to do, and it won't work. This is cattle country. Those farmers have no business squatting in the middle of open range destroying good grazing land with their wheat and corn. We need the railroad, telegraph and telephone lines and open cattle country if we're to achieve statehood in the near future."

"I know all that, but legally . . . ," Smiley said.

"Don't talk to me about legally," Parker said. "When my father came here in fifty-seven, the only legal anything was what he carved out of the land with his own two hands, and I won't

see a bunch of farmers piss on his legacy."

"Well, what do you want us to do, Mr. Parker?" Smiley said. "We can't . . ."

"I'll tell you what I want you to do," Parker said. "I want you to get your two deputies and the three of you ride out to every ranch inside a day's ride and tell them I'm holding a meeting at my place this Saturday. You tell them not attending is not an option. I want you to do it today."

"If all three of us go, that leaves the town unprotected," Smiley said.

"Unprotected from what?" Parker said.

# FIVE

As James and Seth rode into town, Seth hesitated to ask the question that was on his mind. He knew it was disrespectful to question his parents, but his curiosity got the better of him.

"Pa?" Seth said meekly. "There's nothing wrong with the wagon brake."

"I know it," James said.

"You lied to Ma?" Seth said.

"I did."

"But you always said lying is wrong and that we should always tell the truth."

"I know I said that."

"I don't understand."

"Son, there are certain exceptions to every rule."

"You mean there are times when it's all right to lie?"

"I would say that there are times when it's all right to spare someone's feelings by not telling them the truth or to spare them embarrassment. Do you happen to know what this Saturday is?"

Seth thought about it and couldn't come up with an answer to the question. "No, Pa, I don't."

"This Saturday is your ma's birthday," James said.

"I clean forgot."

"I think your ma did too," James said. "So we're going to remind her."

"How?"

30

"I ordered your ma the prettiest blue dress in the catalog from back east and we're going to town to pick it up," James said. "I couldn't very well tell her that and ruin the surprise, so I made up the story about the brake. The other thing is I invited the neighbors over this Saturday to celebrate with a surprise party. So I hope you forgive me for telling that little fib."

"Jeeze, Pa, won't Ma be surprised," Seth said, feeling excitement mounting in his stomach. "I've never seen a party before."

"Tomorrow you come to the field early and help me build a long table to set the food and such on," James said. "We have to hide it from your mother. And don't you dare say one word of any of it to your ma."

"No, Pa, I promise."

"And don't say anything about the brake," James said.

"No, sir," Seth said and grinned. "A party."

Parker was looking out the window of his office when he spotted James Johansen and his boy ride into town on their buckboard wagon. Johansen parked the wagon in front of the general store.

Parker turned and looked at Smiley.

"Before you ride out with your deputies, I just saw James Johansen ride into town," Parker said. "Tell him I'd like a word with him."

"All right, Mr. Parker," Smiley said.

James locked the wagon in place and then helped Seth down to the street. The sidewalk was busy with folks walking to and fro, and a good crowd had gathered inside the general store.

Before they entered the store, Sheriff Smiley approached them from across the street.

"Mr. Johansen," Smiley said.

"Sheriff," James said.

"Mr. Parker would like a word with you," Smiley said.

"What about?"

"He didn't say."

James looked across the street and saw Parker at the window in his office.

"All right, I'll see Mr. Parker," James said. "Seth, I want you to go inside the general store and wait for me by the counter. Tell Mr. Tobey I'll be along directly."

"Okay, Pa."

James crossed the street and walked to Parker's office and opened the door. Parker was standing beside a woodstove with a cup of coffee in his hand.

"You wanted to see me?" James said.

"May I offer you some coffee?" Parker said.

"No thanks," James said. "My boy is waiting on me."

"I'll come right to the point, then," Parker said. "I would like to buy your farm. I'll give you a fair price and a closing bonus."

"Now why would you want to do that?" James said.

"I need the land," Parker said.

"For what?"

"This is cattle country, Mr. Johansen," Parker said. "Cattle require a great deal of land and water. Farms use a great deal of land and water. You can see the dilemma for the ranchers having less and less land as more farmers move into the territory."

"Mr. Parker, what do you have, twenty, twenty-five thousand acres?" James said. "I have a hundred and sixty. I fail to see how I pose a problem to you or any other rancher."

"Five years ago there wasn't one farm in the territory," Parker said. "Today there are fifteen. A year from now there will be twenty-five. Those farms shrink the land, and less land means less cattle. You can see that, can't you?"

"How much money and land does one man need, Mr. Parker?" James said.

Parker felt his fiery temper start to get the better of him. "It isn't a question of need, damn you. It's a question of rights. When I came here in fifty-seven with my father, there was nothing, not even a town worth spit. We built a ranch, this town, a charter of the Cattlemen's Association, and now there's an eye on statehood. You farmers just don't belong here. Now my offer to buy still stands."

"No one is belittling what you and the others who followed you did here," James said. "But you talk as if you and no one else has any rights. Territory or state, this is a free country and my land was bought and paid for proper and legal. And I'll tell you something else. This is my home. There is where my son will grow to a man. There should be a school and a proper church in this town, and there isn't. Why is that, Mr. Parker? Why is there a saloon filled with saloon girls, but not a school and church?"

"I'm a reasonable man, Johansen," Parker said. "But my patience has limits."

"Good day, Mr. Parker," James said.

Seth stood by the candy counter eyeing the gum balls, jawbreakers and candy sticks when James walked into the general store. Mr. Tobey was cutting dress cloth for a woman in the clothing aisle. James stood beside Seth.

"See any you like?" James said.

"All of them."

"Here's two cents," James said and gave Seth two pennies. "When Mr. Tobey comes over, you ask him for what you want."

"Thanks, Pa."

Tobey and the woman from the clothing aisle came to the counter, where the woman paid him for her dress cloth.

"Mr. Johansen, I have your package right here," Tobey said.

Tobey lifted a brown paper package from under the counter

and set it on the countertop.

"It's wrapped, Pa," Seth said.

"I can unwrap it if you want to see it," Tobey said.

"I want to see it," Seth said.

James nodded.

Tobey removed the bow and opened the brown paper and then held up the blue dress in front of the counter.

"It's really pretty, Pa," Seth said.

"And your mother will look really pretty wearing it," Tobey said.

"Do you have any fancy wrap instead of that brown paper?" James said.

"Gift wrap is two cents," Tobey said.

"I'll pay for it, Pa," Seth said and placed his two pennies on the counter.

"That's your candy pennies," James said.

"Ma is more important than candy," Seth said.

"So she is," James said. "Gift wrap, Mr. Tobey."

Tobey selected a golden colored paper with silver trim running through it and wrapped the dress carefully and sealed the package with a bow. "I forgot to mention that a free candy stick comes with the gift wrap," he said.

When James and Seth left the general store, two men were standing beside their wagon. They had the hard look of veteran cowboys. James placed the package on the front seat and lifted Seth into the seat beside the package.

"Something I can help you with?" James said to the two men.

"Couldn't help notice you got a bad wheel," one of the cowboys said.

Each cowboy carried a Colt revolver in a side holster, but as almost every man in town carried one, that was not unusual to James.

"You're Parker's men, aren't you?" James said.

"What of it?" a cowboy said.

"There's nothing wrong with the wagon, but you can tell Parker for me I'm touched by his concern," James said.

James mounted the seat and, as he drove the wagon out of town, he didn't need to look at Parker's office window to know that Parker was watching him.

# SIX

On Saturday morning Seth was so filled with excitement he could barely contain himself as he did his chores. Noon was the time Pa said the guests would start to arrive and he felt he would bust open waiting for the hours to pass.

Pa rode out to the fields as usual, but that was to bring back the table for the party. If he didn't go, Ma would suspect something was wrong. Seth knew he wouldn't be able to hold it in any longer and spoil the secret Pa worked so hard to keep.

After feeding the chickens, milking the cow and bringing her to the corral, cleaning the stalls and gathering up the eggs, Seth decided to help Ma in the house and volunteered to churn the butter.

It took a while to churn the cream into butter. When it finally set, he took the new butter to the icehouse to keep fresh for later.

Ma was in the house mending Pa's shirts when, on his way back from the icehouse, Seth spotted Pa coming home along the road. A dozen wagons were behind Pa's. Seth rushed into the house so quickly he startled Ma and she pricked her finger with the sewing needle.

"Seth, what in the world is . . . ?" Sarah said.

"Ma, come outside quick," Seth said and raced back onto the porch.

Sarah came onto the porch and stood beside Seth as James

and a long train of wagons arrived in a circle in front of the house.

"James, what is going on here?" Sarah said.

James climbed down off the wagon. "Tell your ma, son," he said.

"It's April seventeenth, Ma," Seth said excitedly. "Your birthday."

The surprise registered on Sarah's face. "My goodness, so it is," she said.

"Come on everybody, let's get things set up," James said.

The celebration lasted well into the late afternoon. Fifteen families brought enough food to feed a small army. Fried chicken, Swedish meatballs, roasted hens, potatoes, corn on the cob, carrots, ribs and chops and a dozen or more pies, apple, cherry and peach.

Seth did his best to sample all of it and fell just short of a bellyache. Sarah changed into her new blue dress. Although she blushed at the compliments tossed her way, Seth could see she was pleased with Pa's gift.

Mr. Uggla played his fiddle and another man accompanied him on the harmonica, and the adults danced the afternoon away. No one seemed to notice or care about the skin color of the Jones family, least of all Seth and the other children. Mr. Jones constructed a kite made of wood sticks and paper with a long tail of red-and-blue ribbon. Seth had read about Benjamin Franklin's kite in Ma's book, but had never seen one work before. Mr. Jones took his son, Seth and the other boys into the field beside the house and showed them how to launch the kite into the wind and hold it steady by the long string attached to the wood base. Mr. Jones explained that when he was a slave in Georgia, he learned to make kites from the slaves' assigned woodworking.

Seth, Mr. Jones's son Cal, and the other boys and girls spent the afternoon sailing the kite hundreds of feet in the air.

Late in the afternoon, while the pies and coffee were being served, James proposed a toast to Sarah.

"I may be a bit biased on the subject, but I feel no man ever had a prettier, more loving wife than the good Lord blessed me with," James said. "Happy birthday, hon."

Sarah blushed again as the crowd of neighbors clapped and cheered.

Late in the afternoon, Seth left the field to use the outhouse and he was about to return to the field when he noticed the men were all huddled inside the barn. They were talking in soft hushed tones. Seth knew he wasn't supposed to spy on adults, but he couldn't help himself and hid behind the open barn door.

Pa was telling about the meeting he had with Mr. Parker in Mr. Parker's office. It caused the men to grumble and complain.

Mr. Uggla said, "I seen his men spying on me from a distance. Just watching like a mountain cat watches his prey."

"We all seen that," another man said. "What can we do about it?"

"I know what I'll do about it and that's pack iron," Mr. Pettibone said.

"Now hold on, Pettibone," Pa said. "Before we go off half-cocked, let's think about what laws have been broke. No one has trespassed on my land or threatened me in any way. Have they done so to anyone else?"

No one spoke up and Pa said, "So it seems to me that Parker is trying to throw a scare into us is all. If we stick together and show him we ain't afraid of him, his only recourse is to break the law. If he does that, we have every right to take legal means."

"With who?" Pettibone said. "That bought-and-paid-for Smiley?"

"No, the US marshal out of Casper," Pa said.

"I'll agree to that," Uggla said. "I think most of us will."

"May I say something?" Mr. Jones said.

Seth peered through the slight opening at the edge of the barn door.

"Of course you can, Mal," Pa said. "You're one of us, ain't you?"

"I agree that Mr. Parker is trying to scare us," Mr. Jones said. "Fear is a very powerful weapon for one man to use against another. Back before the war ended, the plantation had three hundred slaves working the fields with just ten white men to control us. Ten against three hundred, and do you know how those ten controlled us? They put the fear of God into each and every one of us. Fear that if we ran off, a dozen hounds would track us down and rip our throats out. Or if we disobeyed, a whipping with a twelve-foot-long whip with an iron tip would follow. Once you put fear into a man, he belongs to you forever. I say the thing to do is to stick together and show Mr. Parker we're not afraid of him, and that we mean to stay put on our own land."

"Any man disagree with that?" Pa said.

No one did. Seth wanted to stay and hear more but Ma had snuck up behind him and gave him a good whack on the behind.

"We'll talk about spying on adults later," Ma said. "Right now go help your friends pack up to leave."

"Yes, Ma," Seth said.

Before everyone left, they gathered in a circle to wish Sarah a happy birthday one more time.

Then James had some parting words.

"I'd like to make a suggestion to everyone," James said. "Last Fourth of July, some of us went to town and others did not. I would like to suggest that we hold our own celebration at one of our homes this year. If everyone is agreeable, I'd like to nominate Mr. Jones and his family to be our first host."

Fourteen families agreed.

"I . . . I . . . ," Mal Jones stammered.

"Before my husband steps on his tongue, we accept," Keri Jones said.

There was a loud cheer. Seth cheered the loudest.

# SEVEN

Every rancher within a day's ride of the Parker ranch made the trip for the meeting he'd planned. Parker's only son, John, greeted each rancher as they rode up and escorted them into the large den where the meeting was to be held.

When all were present, seated, served coffee, brandy and cigars, Parker called the meeting to order.

"Gentlemen, all of us are cattlemen here, and I appreciate all of you showing up to support our noble efforts," Parker said. "Wyoming is less than a decade away from statehood. That is something I thought I would never see in my lifetime. However, our very livelihood is threatened even as I stand here and speak. I'm not talking about another drought like the one we had seven years ago. I am talking about the encroachment of the farmers. Inside of a half a day's ride around my land there are fifteen farms between one hundred and two hundred acres in size. By eighty-five, that number will have doubled, and our open range will have shrunk. I would like to hear your thoughts on this subject."

The meeting raged on for an hour, with each rancher speaking his mind. All agreed that statehood was coming and cattlemen were leading the charge. All agreed the growing number of farmers was a concern to all of them. They also agreed that as long as the territory allowed farmers to buy land, there didn't seem to be anything they could do about it.

"I was thinking we should sign and take a petition to the territorial governor to ask for a hold on land for sale to farmers," Parker said. "If we could slow down their growth until statehood arrives and the Cattlemen's Association becomes more powerful in the state, we can practically eliminate the farmer altogether. We can ask the Santa Fe to bring the railroad here to move our cattle and eliminate the months a trail drive requires. They will do it if we are one hundred percent cattle country."

Jim Klum, one of Parker's closest neighbors, said, "And who takes this petition to the governor?"

"All of your land put together in this room doesn't add up to half my spread," Parker said. "That makes me the most powerful person in this room. However, when the time comes, any who wish to make the trip to see the governor are welcome to join me."

"Us fifteen doesn't seem enough," Klum said.

"And you are correct," Parker said. "My son John here and a group of my men will spend the summer months riding across the territory in all four directions to get the signature of every rancher, no matter how large or small, on the petition. When we present it to the territorial governor he will have no choice but to listen to our demands. All in favor, raise your hands. All not in favor you are free to leave with no hard feelings."

At the conclusion of the meeting Parker had the signature of every man in the room on the petition and he locked it away in his safe.

Then Parker and his son took coffee, brandy and fresh cigars out to the porch to watch the sunset as they did most every evening.

"The men tell me the farmers had a big shindig at the Johansen place today," John said.

"I got word," Parker said. "It was Sarah Johansen's birthday."

"Pa, all this business with signatures and such, why not let me handle this in my own way?" John said. "No man has ever beaten me with fist or gun, you know that."

"And how would it look when statehood arrives and I run to be its first governor if I have a son in prison for murder?" Parker said. "This is not the time for gunplay. If and when that time does arrive, I will hire it out discreetly so our hands stay nice and clean. Do you understand me, boy?"

"Yes, sir."

"Now, first of May you take a dozen men and head out in all directions and get as many signatures as possible in a month's time," Parker said. "I plan to bring the governor the petition at the Fourth of July celebration in Casper. As many signatures as possible."

"And the farmers?" John said.

"Keep up the surveillance, but from a distance and by no means are you or any of the men to engage them," Parker said. "We just want to let them know of our presence. That's all we want to do at this time."

"What if one of them engages us?" John said.

"If they start something, then by all means finish it," Parker said. "But no gunplay and no killings. Understand?"

"Sure, Pa," John said.

"Tell the men to concentrate their efforts on Johansen," Parker said. "He's the leader. If he falls, they all fall."

"Sure, Pa." John grinned.

# EIGHT

Two days of steady rain put a temporary stop to plowing the fields for the spring planting. James kept busy around the farm sharpening axes and tools, repairing odd and ends and tending the leather hides he'd been meaning to get around to but just didn't have the time to tend to.

Seth did all of his regular chores and schoolwork so he wasn't underfoot, so James had plenty of spare time to work out the details in his mind on how he planned to talk to Sarah about expanding the farm.

The second day of rain the sky cleared right around supper-time. After supper, James asked Sarah to the porch to talk about a few things and assigned Seth dishwashing duty to keep him from overhearing.

James carried out two cups of coffee and his pipe. He took the time to stuff the pipe bowl full and get a good burn going as he stalled to find the right words.

Sarah, nobody's fool, knew her husband oh, so well, and said, "James, all the stalling in the world isn't going to get the words off your tongue."

"Now don't rush me, hon," James said. "I'm working up to it."

"Work up to it a little faster," Sarah said. "The sun is going down and I don't want to be sitting here when it comes up."

"Don't get riled, honey, and listen to what I have to say," James said.

"I will, provided you say it soon," Sarah said.

"I told you I spoke with Mr. Wilson at the bank," James said.

"James," Sarah said.

"Now just listen to me for a minute," James said. "We can get that land, all one hundred and sixty acres for twelve hundred dollars, and double the size of our farm and production and build on our future."

"We don't have twelve hundred dollars," Sarah said. "We have three hundred."

"If we write our folks, mine and yours, and ask them to lend us the money, I'm sure between all the cousins, sisters and brothers they could raise nine hundred dollars," James said. "Once I have that soil turned and worked, we can pay them all back with interest in three years. Seth is almost grown enough to work a plow, and if I have to I'll work seven days a week. The thing is, honey, it's for us and Seth and someday for his wife and family. The only way to prosper in these times is to expand production, and I can't do that without expanding our land. You see that I'm making sense, don't you?"

"What kind of interest, James?" Sarah said.

"I'll ask Mr. Wilson to calculate that," James said.

"I suppose you'll want me to write the letters?" Sarah said.

"If you wouldn't mind," James said. "You write so much better than me."

"I'll write them tomorrow," Sarah said. "But you must do something for me first."

"Name it."

"Send Seth to bed early tonight."

"Why?"

"My temperature is up."

"Are you sick?"

"No."

"I don't understand."

"Send Seth to bed early and I'll explain it to you," Sarah said, stood up and went inside.

James worked it out in his mind and when it came to him he stood up. "Hey, wait for me," he said.

# NINE

By the third week of May, James had eighty acres seeded, and sprouts of corn and wheat were popping up through the earth. A good supply of rain, sun and manure assured him the crop would be bumper.

For a few days early in the month, Parker's men stood on the hill watching him, but after the first week they didn't come around again.

Then the letter arrived from Wisconsin. The entire family had put together the money needed to buy the land. Someone had a sense of humor about it, because the amount raised was nine hundred and one dollars wired directly to the bank.

When Sarah read the letter at dinner, James could barely contain his excitement at the news.

The following morning after he checked the fields, James, Sarah and Seth rode to town to see Mr. Wilson.

Wilson prepared the transfer papers and deed and, after the money in their account was drawn, he required James and Sarah sign two copies of each.

The land was theirs.

All one hundred and sixty acres of prime bottomland.

James celebrated the event by taking Seth and Sarah to lunch at the hotel restaurant where he spent two dollars and seventy cents on the meals. Then they rode back to the farm to inspect their new land.

"It's real pretty land, Pa," Seth said.

"And it's going to be a great deal of work to turn pretty to useful," Sarah said.

"Not so much with my son helping me," James said.

"Can I, Pa?" Seth said.

"You bet you can."

"We'll start tomorrow," James said. "Me and my boy, by God, will have this land ready for fall harvest."

"His schoolwork will not suffer, James," Sarah said.

"Now Sarah, even in the big cities they take the summer months off from school and the books," James said.

"Pa's right," Seth said.

"And how would you know?" Sarah scolded Seth. She looked at James. "What will you plant and how will you pay for seed?"

"Mr. Tobey will extend us credit for seed," James said. "And what do people eat the most come fall for Thanksgiving besides turkey?"

"I know, Pa," Seth said. "Pumpkin pie. People always have pumpkin pie at Thanksgiving, right?"

"And squash," James said. "And we're going to plant forty acres of each."

Sarah looked at the unturned one hundred and sixty acres. "Do you think it will work, James?"

"We'll make it work," James said.

"Then I will be helping in the field," Sarah said.

"Now, hon, a field is no place for a woman," James said.

"Rubbish," Sarah said. "You forget that I spent many a year on my father's farm behind a plow team. I'll not sit around the house mending socks while my men are toiling in the sun if I can help it, and I will."

Seth looked at James, waiting for his pa to scold his ma into submission. Instead James put his arm around Sarah and smiled.

"We best get you some pants," James said.

# TEN

"You did what, you stupid son of a bitch?" Parker said to Wilson when the banker told Parker of the Johansen sale of the one hundred and sixty acres.

They were in the saloon at the bar, and at the sound of Parker's raised voice a hush fell across the room.

Wilson, about to sip from his beer mug, slowly set it upon the bar, turned and looked at Parker.

"You have no right to speak to me that way," Wilson said. "You asked about the one hundred and sixty acres, and I told you as a matter of public record."

Parker softened a bit and patted Wilson on the back. "You're right, of course, and I apologize for my language. It's just these farmers upset me to the point I let my temper get the better of me."

"I do understand how you feel," Wilson said. "But they have every right to buy land that's for sale and farm on it. The same rights as you have for ranching. The two will just have to coexist as best you can."

"And when the Santa Fe passes us by and statehood gets pushed back another decade, what then?" Parker said.

"You don't know that for sure," Wilson said. "People do eat more than just beef, Mr. Parker, and it has to be shipped as well. Horse and cart doesn't get it back east quick enough anymore. Perhaps the Santa Fe might want to look at moving produce and in doing so decide to build her and then you can take advantage of that move as well."

"Well, that is something to think about," Parker said.

Wilson sipped from his beer and then set it down. "If you'll excuse me, I have to close the bank," he said.

"Again, I'm sorry for my language," Parker said.

Wilson nodded and left the saloon.

Parker turned and looked at the table where his ranch foreman Teasel and a few hands were drinking beers. He walked to the table and looked at Teasel.

"A word with you in my office when you're done with your beer," Parker said.

Teasel was an excellent foreman and trail boss. Tough as a nickel steak, good with a gun and totally fearless in his job, Teasel was a valuable commodity to have on his side.

"You wanted to see me, Mr. Parker?" Teasel said when he entered Parker's office.

"Yes. Have a seat," Parker said.

Teasel sat, pulled out a tobacco pouch and rolling paper and fixed a cigarette.

"Where is my son at the moment?" Parker said.

"South, on the way to Rock Springs with some of the men," Teasel said. "He said he'd be gone about ten days collecting signatures."

Parker nodded. "I don't want to pull you away from your duties too much, but I need you to do something for me."

Teasel struck a match on his boot and lit the cigarette. "Anything you say, Mr. Parker."

"Take some of the boys around to visit the farmers," Parker said. "Don't trespass or threaten, but have some fun at their expense. See if maybe you can get a few of them to lose their temper. Start with Pettibone. He's a hothead. A few assault charges filed against these farmers might swing the way folks in town think about them to our way."

"What about Johansen?" Teasel said. "He seems to be the leader of these farmers. I heard you in the saloon say he's doubled the size of his place."

"He's too smart for that," Parker said. "It would take a lot more than some heckling to rile his feathers."

"All right," Teasel said. He hesitated and then said, "Can I suggest something?"

"What?"

"Seems to be getting one of them to start a fight out in the fields isn't going to do much good without witnesses," Teasel said. "Why not provoke them into a fight here in town where people can see it? Most of them come into town on Saturday for supplies. It won't take much to get Pettibone to throw a fist."

"Excellent idea," Parker said. "And even better is to let Pettibone win the fight and do some damage we can file charges on and have Smiley lock him up."

"I'll have one of the boys do it," Teasel said. "No one would believe a farmer took me with his fists."

Parker nodded. "What do I pay you as foreman?"

"Sixty a month," Teasel said.

"Let's make it seventy-five," Parker said.

# ELEVEN

Wearing blue dungarees, a white shirt, boots, sun hat and work gloves, Sarah drove the team through the ground as she had done for years back in Wisconsin on her father's farm.

It was hot, but the team was strong, and she had to control their desire to rip through the dirt and ruin the straight pattern necessary for planting.

Behind Sarah, Seth picked up rocks and tossed them into the wagon hauled by James. Every once in a while a rock would be too big for Seth to handle and James would come around and place it into the cart. When the cart was full, James would haul it off the field and dump it into a pile.

Shirtless, as James pulled the heavy cart the muscles in his arms, his chest and shoulders appeared to burst through his skin.

Seth thought his pa the strongest man in the world as he watched him haul the cart full of rocks.

Around noon, Sarah fed and watered the team while James hauled a full cart to the growing pile.

Then they ate a picnic lunch in the shade of a tree.

"I think we can get two more acres in by three o'clock," James said. "Then you and Seth take the team home for the day. Seth, you rub them down good and use the liniment on their legs. I don't want them getting sore. I'll stay behind a bit and finish clearing rocks."

"How much have we done, Pa?" Seth said.

"Looks to be about ten acres," James said.

"We have a long way to go," Seth said.

"Remember, we're only clearing eighty acres for planting this year," James said. "We'll make it in plenty of time."

"How do we plant squash and pumpkin, Pa?" Seth asked.

"With seed," James said. "Squash requires a bit of care getting in the ground, but this time of year should be no problem. The pumpkin seeds will grow and spread out, which is why less are planted. Forty acres should produce a whole lot for market. Both should be ready by late September or early October."

"Pa, can we keep a few pumpkins for jack-o'-lanterns?" Seth said.

"I don't see why not, provided we keep a few for your ma's pumpkin pies," James said.

"We'll keep nothing unless we get back to work and ready the field," Sarah said.

Around three thirty in the afternoon, Sarah and Seth took the team home and James stayed behind to gather up rocks from the field. The pile of rocks was high enough he could build a stone house or wall out of them, and there were seventy acres left to go.

He had an idea, though. He would use the rocks to build a large outdoor oven and barbecue pit so they could roast and cook outside in the summer. That way the interior of the house wasn't always a hundred degrees.

All he needed was the rocks, which he had, and some bags of cement, which he could order from Mr. Tobey at the general store.

Just past four thirty, James dumped the last cart of rocks for the day, put on his shirt and headed for home.

Three cowboys were on the hill to his right. They appeared to be following him. Parker's men looking for a fight, James thought. He wouldn't give them what they wanted.

They rode up closer.

"I was wondering if you knew the time?" one of them said. "I seem to've forgot my watch."

"I don't own a watch," James said as he kept walking.

"Seems to me it might be time for a bath," another cowboy said. "As I seem to smell pig."

"How does that pretty wife of yours stand that stink?" the third cowboy sneered.

At the mention of Sarah, James felt his temper rise. He turned to face the cowboys, but they laughed and rode away.

He would have to watch his temper and not give Parker the upper hand in this, James thought. A fight was what Parker was after, and a fight was something he would not get.

After supper, James and Sarah took coffee on the porch and James smoked his pipe. After washing the dishes, Seth was allowed to join them.

"We should have all eighty acres ready before the first of June," James said. "I've lost track of the days. What is today?"

"Tuesday, Pa," Seth said.

"So it is," James said. "This Saturday you and your ma ride in to see Mr. Tobey and pick up our seeds. We'll store them in the barn away from the sun where it's cool. By Saturday you'll be ahead of me by five or six acres, and I'll haul rocks while you go to town."

Seth looked at Sarah.

"Yes, Seth, you may get some penny candy," Sarah said.

# TWELVE

Seth could barely contain his excitement at riding into town on Saturday to pick up the seeds. It was the first time ever he went to town without Pa, and it made him feel like he was grown up enough to be trusted to protect Ma.

From who or what, Seth had no idea, but the notion of it made him feel almost like a grown man.

The general store was busy, as it always was on Saturday. They had to wait their turn right behind Mr. Pettibone, who was picking up wire for a new chicken coop. Seth kept himself occupied by looking over the various jars of candy at the candy counter.

Then Mr. Pettibone carried out his wire, and Ma was next.

That's when the trouble started.

Dusty was a pretty good cowboy. Able-bodied, smart, and he followed orders. Teasel selected him to pick the fight with Pettibone. Dusty agreed to allow the farmer to beat him with his fists in order to help Mr. Parker, provided Mr. Parker didn't forget the favor.

When Pettibone carried out his wire to put into his wagon, Dusty was seated in a chair on the porch of the general store. He extended his right leg and tripped Pettibone down the steps and into the street.

Pettibone landed in fresh horse chips. When he got up, his temper got the better of him and he was furious.

"Watch where you're going, pig farmer," Dusty said. "Them is new boots you stepped on."

"You tripped me," Pettibone said.

"You tripped yourself," Dusty said. "And scuffed my new boots. Why don't you come here and clean them off for me?"

"You're a liar," Pettibone said.

Dusty stood up from his chair.

"Prove it," Dusty said.

"I ain't carrying iron," Pettibone said.

Dusty removed his gun belt and set it on the chair. "Me neither," he said.

Pettibone charged up the steps and swung wildly at Dusty.

Dusty could see right off that Pettibone, despite his explosive temper, had no real notion of how to fight. Dusty figured he would carry the man for a few minutes.

Dusty allowed Pettibone to trade blows, and then they grabbed each other by the shoulders and engaged in a shoving match.

By now people were starting to gather around to watch.

"You men stop that!" someone shouted.

Dusty broke free and punched Pettibone in the nose. The farmer backed up until his head struck the window of the general store, cracking it in a spiderweb pattern.

Dusty backed off and allowed Pettibone to gather himself. Then Dusty threw two roundhouse punches that deliberately missed.

"You men stop this at once!" Tobey shouted from the door of the general store. "Look what you did to my window."

Dusty let fly with another right hook that glanced off Pettibone's jaw.

"Come on, pig farmer, before you get hurt why don't you . . . ?" Dusty said.

Pettibone charged Dusty and tossed a powerful punch that

caught Dusty flat-footed and sent him flying off the porch and directly into the hitching post in the street. A dozen people watched in horror as Dusty's neck struck the thick rail of the post, snapping the rail in two upon impact.

Collectively there was a loud gasp from the gathered crowd.

"Seth, look away!" Sarah shouted from the open door of the general store.

"Somebody get the sheriff!" a voice in the crowd shouted.

"I didn't mean it," Pettibone said. "It was an accident. I didn't mean it."

Sheriff Smiley raced to the general store from his office across the street and knelt down in front of Dusty.

"This man is dead," Smiley said.

"I didn't mean it," Pettibone said. "It was an accident."

From his office window Parker and Teasel watched the fight unfold.

"It looks like Dusty has done us a big favor in getting himself killed like that," Parker said.

"He was a good man," Teasel said.

"Then let's not let his murder go to waste," Parker said. "Go out there and identify Dusty to Smiley as one of my men."

"Does he have any kin I can notify?" Smiley said from behind his desk.

"Sister in Missouri he talked about," Teasel said. "I don't know about his folks."

"Never mind that now," Parker said. "I want that farmer charged with the murder of my cowhand. Is that clear, Sheriff?"

"I'll have to get word to the circuit judge and federal marshal in Casper," Smiley said.

"You do that," Parker said. "In the meantime that farmer stays locked up tight in your jail. Understand?"

57

"He's a family man," Smiley said.

"Who murdered my hand in cold blood with his fists in front of a dozen or more witnesses," Parker said. "He stays in jail until a circuit judge says otherwise."

"That could be a week to ten days," Smiley said.

"Sheriff Smiley, Dusty was a very popular hand with my men," Parker said. "If you let that farmer return home pending his trial, some of my men may take it upon themselves to pay him a visit at his farm, if you understand me."

"It might be best he stays here at that," Smiley said.

"I think that would be wise," Parker said.

After loading the crates of seeds onto the wagon, Sarah and Seth went into the sheriff's office to speak to Smiley.

"I'm sorry, Mrs. Johansen, but there is nothing I can do until a circuit judge and federal marshal arrive," Smiley said.

"But I clearly saw it all," Sarah said. "That man provoked a fight, and Pettibone gave him one. That he struck his head on the hitching post was nothing but an accident. Pettibone was simply defending himself in a fair fight."

"Would you be willing to write a statement to such and testify at the trial?" Smiley said.

"I and many others, I'm sure," Sarah said.

"I saw it, too," Seth said.

"Seth, be quiet. You're too young," Sarah said.

Smiley opened a desk drawer and removed an official paper used for statements. "Take this home and write your statement on it and return it to me as soon as you can," he said.

"Thank you," Sarah said. "I will."

"Pettibone? They can't do that," James said, after Sarah told him the news.

"They did do it, James, and I'm afraid there isn't much we

can do about it until a judge and marshal arrive," Sarah said.

"Pettibone is a hothead, that's for sure, but he ain't a murderer," James said.

"I know it, and I'll say so at the trial," Sarah said. "Seth, fetch the ink and pen so I can write my statement."

Seth went to the chest where his schoolbooks, paper tablet, pencils, ink bottle and pen were stored and took the pen and ink bottle to the table.

"This is Parker's doing," James said. "I'd bet my life on it."

"Mr. Parker was nowhere around at the time, James," Sarah said.

"A scorpion is nowhere around either," James said, "until he stings you."

# THIRTEEN

James, Sarah and Seth rode out to the Pettibone farm the Saturday after the fight. Pettibone was still being held in jail without bail, and the official word from Casper was that a circuit judge and marshal would arrive on Monday's Overland Stage.

Rachel, Pettibone's wife of fourteen years, was distraught but did her best to put on a gracious face for her guests. She served tea and cake on the porch while Seth played with her two sons in the front yard.

"My husband has always had a temper, but he has never raised a hand to me or the boys or spoken a cruel word in anger," Rachel said.

"We know that," James told her. "And everyone else will know it, too, when he has his day in court. Sarah will testify on his behalf, as will other witnesses."

"It will work out," Sarah said. "You'll see."

"And if it doesn't?" Rachel said. "What happens to me and my sons?"

US Marshal Harper and Circuit Court Judge Miller arrived together by stagecoach on Monday mid-morning. They spent most of the day and half the night reviewing evidence and witness statements in order to determine if there was enough evidence to charge Pettibone with first-degree murder.

Miller made the decision to charge Pettibone with assault, battery and negligent homicide. Harper spent Tuesday lining up the witnesses for and against Pettibone, and then made the arrangements to use the saloon for the trial on Wednesday.

On the Tuesday stagecoach, two attorneys from Casper arrived in town. Mr. Cox for the defense and Mr. Gosney for the prosecution. Both men worked for the circuit court and were there at the request of Judge Miller. They spent the afternoon with Judge Miller reviewing all evidence and statements to prepare their cases for trial and selecting twelve members for the jury.

The trial began at ten o'clock on Wednesday morning in the saloon. Tables and chairs were set up for the judge, defense and prosecution. Nearly every citizen in the town of Brooks attended.

As a witness, Sarah was allowed to sit front row with James. Seth was not allowed inside, but he and dozens of other boys crowded around the door and windows.

Gosney did an excellent job prosecuting the case, and Cox did an excellent job defending it. Sarah was on the witness stand for thirty minutes and gave a good account of what she saw and heard. She held up well under harsh questioning from Gosney.

Pettibone was allowed to testify on his own behalf and, while he did admit to losing his temper, he said it was for good cause at having been deliberately tripped by Dusty. Cox was unable to bring forth a single witness to back up Pettibone's story.

In his closing argument, Gosney gave the jury three things to think about while deciding upon a verdict.

The first was that it was well-known by everyone in town that Pettibone had an explosive temperament.

The second was that not one witness could claim they knew if Dusty tripped Pettibone on purpose or if Pettibone, blinded by the large bail of wire he was carrying, simply tripped on Dusty's boots and flew into a rage, as his temper so often got

61

the better of him.

The third thing was the fact that dozens of witnesses saw Pettibone beat Dusty with his fists, knocking the cowboy off the porch and into the hitching post and to his death.

The jury retired at four in the afternoon.

At eight in the evening they returned with a verdict of guilty.

Judge Miller sentenced Pettibone to three years hard labor at the Yuma Penitentiary in Arizona Territory. Marshal Harper would escort Pettibone to Yuma on Thursday morning.

On Thursday morning at seven o'clock sharp, Pettibone said good-bye to Rachel and his sons and was placed in irons before boarding the stagecoach with Miller.

The last thing Pettibone saw out the coach window as it rode out of town was Rachel fainting into the arms of his sons.

# FOURTEEN

Parker waited one week after the trial to visit Rachel Pettibone. He made the trip by carriage. His son John, back from Casper, went with him.

Rachel served tea in the modest parlor and sent the boys outside to play while she attended to her visitors.

"I will come right to it, Mrs. Pettibone," Parker said. "You are in a bad way here. Your man is gone for three years and you can't work this farm alone. If you could find a qualified man to work your fields, what you would need to pay him would leave you with nothing to live on come this winter. I'm prepared to buy this farm and give you a fair price for it. That would allow you to move to Arizona Territory and live comfortably while you wait for your husband to serve out his three years. I will give you one thousand dollars in cash for the deed."

Rachel watched Parker carefully while the man spoke, didn't interrupt, and waited until he was finished to reply.

"Mr. Parker," Rachel said. "I cannot prove it, but I deeply suspect that you had your man deliberately pick a fight with my husband. That it ended the way that it did was an accident, of that I am sure, but you were behind it nonetheless. The price for this farm is three thousand dollars in cash."

"That's rather steep, isn't it?" Parker said.

"My husband is forty years old," Rachel said. "He is in perfect health and will probably live another twenty years. This farm turns a profit of three hundred dollars a year. Do the math as I have. My price is three thousand dollars. Take it or leave it. I don't care which."

"Stop by my office in town tomorrow morning, and I'll have the money ready for you," Parker said. "And bring the deed."

Riding back to town, John said, "Three thousand is kind of steep for some dirt, isn't it, Pa?"

"I was prepared to go five," Parker said. "And it isn't just some dirt, John. It's a beginning."

In his office in town, Parker reviewed the signed petitions gathered by his son and the other hands he sent out to gather them.

"Thirty-seven names is a good start, but it's not enough," Parker said. "Did any refuse to sign?"

"No," John said.

"We need one hundred signatures," Parker said. "You will have to go west and then south. I want you and the men to leave tomorrow first light."

"Pa, it's almost June," John complained.

"I know the months of the year," Parker said. "And if I'm to bring the petition to the governor in time for the Fourth, you have to go tomorrow and return before the end of June. Understood?"

"Yes, sir."

"Double the amount of men," Parker said. "Teasel can handle things on the ranch."

"Yes, sir," John said.

"Now, let's go home and celebrate our small victory today with a first-class barbecue and hoedown for the men," Parker said.

"Can we bring women?" John said.

"If you must," Parker said. "But no roughhousing, and

nobody gets out of line."

"Wouldn't dream of it, Pa," John said.

# FIFTEEN

Sarah walked among the fields and marveled at the beauty of nature contained and controlled. The corn and the wheat were growing to maturity and would be ready for harvest by summer's end.

The squash and pumpkins, still in their infancy of their cycle, were nonetheless showing all the signs of producing full fields of mature crop by early fall.

It made the blisters on her hands and feet, the aches in her neck and back all worthwhile.

James had proven to be right. She knew the investment of time, labor and money would provide them a better life in the future.

Yet for all the promise the future seemed to hold, there was a sadness in her heart at the fact that she hadn't become pregnant once again.

And not for the lack of trying either.

James and Seth rode to town to pick up some wire for the chicken coop and a barrel of nails and wouldn't return until at least noon.

Sarah needed to go home and prepare lunch for her hungry men.

She also needed to pray that her husband's seed would take root inside her body and produce for him the second son he so desperately wanted and needed.

What better place to pray than in the fields where God had

demonstrated his grace and beauty? So she bowed her head and asked the Almighty for a son.

When Sarah returned from the fields, Rachel Pettibone and her two sons were waiting for her on the porch.

"I have a favor to ask," Rachel said.

"Please stay for lunch," Sarah said. "James and Seth will be back from town shortly and they would love to see you."

"Great fried chicken, Ma," Seth said.

"I have to agree," James said.

"We'll take coffee on the porch and you can tell us your favor," Sarah said to Rachel.

While Seth and Rachel's boys played in the yard, Rachel said, "I'm leaving for Arizona Territory in a few days to settle near the prison to wait for my husband. I've sold the farm to Mr. Parker, and I can't pack the wagon myself. I wonder if you might come over tomorrow to assist me."

"Of course I'll help," James said. "It's the least I can do. And I am so sorry for everything that's happened. I can't say I'm glad to see you and the boys leave, but I certainly do understand it. Will you be hiring a man to make the trip south with you?"

"I have a good shotgun and my husband's pistol," Rachel said. "I'll stay on the marked trails close to the army outposts all the way. We'll be fine."

After Rachel and her sons left, James sat alone on the porch, drank his coffee and smoked his pipe.

Ideas were forming in his mind, and he didn't like the shape they were taking. Parker had got his hands on one farm; what was to stop him from grabbing more until he had them all?

Sheriff Smiley was next to useless. He was little more than Parker's appointed flunky.

James could write the US marshal in Casper and ask him to investigate Parker's business, but with what just cause? He paid for land that was sold to him willingly. One of his hands picked a fight and paid for it with his life, and the man who took the life was gone for three years. Even if Parker was behind it all, what proof did James or anybody else have?

None.

Still, he neither liked nor trusted Parker as far as he could spit.

But as long as Parker didn't break the law, what could he do about it?

He mulled over the one idea that seemed to make sense to him and decided to unveil it at the Fourth of July celebration.

The following morning, James drove Sarah and Seth to the Pettibone farm to help Rachel pack. She had two wagons, one covered, the other a flat cart with two wheels balanced in the center.

They spent the entire morning and into the early afternoon loading certain items of furniture Rachel wanted to keep, cases of canned goods, jerked meat, a fifty-gallon water barrel and trunks of clothing.

By the time Rachel and Sarah served the final lunch ever prepared in the kitchen by Rachel's hand, both wagons were fully loaded.

After lunch, Rachel told Sarah to pick out anything she liked of what was left to keep, as she saw no reason Parker should have it.

James hitched the massive team of plow horses to the wagon.

Then, with some crying on Rachel and Sarah's part, hugs and kisses and promises to write, Rachel drove the wagons off her farm and onto the dirt road.

Sarah went through the house and selected some odds and

ends that she could use or thought a neighbor might want, and she and Seth loaded them onto the wagon.

James took every farming tool and implement the wagon would hold, if not for his own use, then for a neighbor's.

Then, with a final look around the Pettibone farm, James drove his family home.

# SIXTEEN

Away from the ranch, John Parker had a dark, sinister and violent side to him that very few people ever witnessed firsthand. His father kept him in check most of the time, but once set free of his father's reins, the monster inside John took every opportunity to break free and rear its ugly head.

Shaun O'Brien had a very small spread just south of the Montana border near Colby. A hundred head, a few longhorns and not much else. After two weeks in the saddle, John was tired, sore and feeling mean.

A widower, O'Brien had a fifteen-year-old daughter who helped with chores and roundup and was a right stargazer to look at, to boot.

Riding with three men, John split them up when they were east of Colby so they could cover more ranchers.

John rode into the O'Brien spread alone.

O'Brien came out of the house to meet him. O'Brien's daughter stayed on the porch beside the open door.

John didn't dismount but talked to O'Brien from the saddle.

"I'm John Parker. My father is Jefferson Parker and he owns the largest cattle ranch in the territory," John said.

"I met your father once years ago," O'Brien said. "What's your business here?"

"I'm collecting signatures of every rancher in the state to take to Casper in protest against all the farmers moving in," John said.

"I got nothing against farmers," O'Brien said.

"Maybe so, but I need you to sign the petition," John said.

"I won't sign nothing I don't believe in," O'Brien said.

John stared at O'Brien for a moment. Then with cat-like reflexes, he flicked his right boot straight out and kicked O'Brien in the face.

The old rancher fell against the rail in his corral. John quickly dismounted and pulled his Colt .44 pistol.

"Sign," John said.

"No."

John smacked O'Brien three times across the face with the heavy Colt pistol, and O'Brien fell to his knees.

O'Brien's daughter came running down from the porch, but O'Brien held up his hand. "Jessie, stay back!" he yelled.

"Sign," John said.

"You go to hell," O'Brien said.

John removed the two-foot-long leather whip from his saddle horn and whipped O'Brien several times across the face.

"Sign," John demanded.

O'Brien spat blood on John's boots.

John looked at Jessie. "She's right juicy, that daughter of yours. What did you say her name was?"

O'Brien looked up at John. "No, please."

"I bet she's a tomcat once she's warmed up proper," John said.

"Please," O'Brien begged.

"Sign," John demanded.

"I'll sign," O'Brien said. "Just leave my daughter be and I'll sign."

"That wasn't so hard now, was it?" John said.

★ ★ ★ ★ ★

John met up with his men in Colby where they planned to spend the night in the accommodations at the whorehouse above the saloon.

Before heading upstairs to the second floor, John and his men were having a few drinks at a table when the swinging doors burst open and a shotgun-wielding O'Brien burst into the crowded saloon.

"You son of a bitch!" O'Brien yelled. "She's just fifteen!"

O'Brien aimed the shotgun at John. As dozens of men hit the floor, John calmly stood, drew his Colt, cocked it and shot O'Brien dead with one shot to the heart in the blink of an eye.

John holstered the Colt before O'Brien hit the floor.

"Anybody know what this old man was shouting about?" John said.

# SEVENTEEN

Parker was in a fine mood on the afternoon of the Fourth of July. He returned the day before from a trip to Casper, where he presented more than a hundred signatures to the territorial governor in protest over land being sold to farmers.

Besides the petition, Parker was able to tell the governor that the Cattlemen's Association had granted Wyoming a full charter and that as the largest rancher in the territory, he would represent the association in Washington.

The governor all but turned green in the face by the time the meeting ended. Parker returned home feeling no more valuable land would be sold to farmers.

Main Street was closed for the day, and Parker donated two heads of his prime beef for a giant all-invited celebration. He brought his cook into town to supervise the barbecue, and dozens of pies, cakes and breads were baked by townsfolk.

While in Casper, Parker purchased five hundred dollars' worth of fireworks that John and Teasel would set off after dark.

By late afternoon, three hundred people, including most of his hands and the hands of neighboring ranchers, had gathered on Main Street.

Parker watched from the second-floor balcony of the hotel. He sipped from a cold glass of beer and watched as the town's citizens feasted on his beef. He was feeling pretty good about the way things had turned around when he suddenly realized that he didn't see one farmer anywhere in town.

Odd.

Not one. Not a wife or child of a farmer anywhere.

John and Teasel were in the room with him, seated at the dining table where they were reading the instruction booklet on operating the fireworks.

"John, come here a moment," Parker said.

John joined Parker on the balcony.

"Yeah, Pa?" John said.

"Look below. What do you see?"

"A whole bunch of people having a good time," John said.

"Do you see or recognize one farmer or member of a farmer's family anywhere?"

John scanned the crowd, searching faces. Although he knew many of the farmers by sight and some by name, he didn't see a one.

"No, Pa, I don't."

"Odd, don't you think?" Parker said. "That on Independence Day not one of them comes to town to celebrate?"

"Maybe they're afraid to show their faces in town?" John said.

"Something else is going on," Parker said.

Teasel came onto the balcony. "I think I know, Mr. Parker," he said.

"Know what?"

"That new pup we hired on last winter, Jason, all of nineteen, do you know him?" Teasel said.

"Can't say as I do," Parker said.

"I know him," John said.

"So you know him, what of it?" Parker said.

"That farmer named Uggla, the big Swede," Teasel said. "Has a fifteen-year-old daughter Jason's sweet on. I heard Jason talking in the bunkhouse the other day about the farmers were holding their own celebration at the Jones farm, and he was going to sneak over and see the daughter."

"Their own celebration?" Parker said.

"At the Jones farm," Teasel said.

"Has Jason left yet?" Parker said.

"He took off about an hour ago," Teasel said.

"I don't care what time this Jason kid gets back, you bring him to see me," Parker said. "Immediately."

"Sure thing," Teasel said.

John and Teasel returned to the fireworks book and Parker stayed on the balcony. All of a sudden his mood had turned sour, and he knew the root cause of it was the farmers.

Well, soon enough every last one of them would be gone from the valley.

The thought of that cheered him up.

"John, bring me another cold beer," Parker said.

# EIGHTEEN

Although Pettibone and his family were sorely missed, the Fourth of July feast was such a festive occasion and the Jones family such good hosts that everyone's mood was joyful.

The food was overwhelming, with ribs, turkey, beef, carrots, potatoes, breads, cakes and pies. Candy and salted bowls of popcorn sat on each end of the table. Uggla played his fiddle, couples danced; the kids flew kites made by Mal Jones.

After dark, several families brought fireworks, and a fine display was put on. The kids had sparklers. When the show ended, James called the men into the Jones barn to discuss his idea with them.

"After what happened to Pettibone, I got to thinking about something I'd like to talk over with everybody," James said. "I know we're a small community here in the valley with just fourteen farms, but in the entire territory there must be fifty or even seventy-five farms out there. I think we should contact Minneapolis, or maybe even send a few of us to the Grange headquarters they have there and ask to become members. If we can become part of the Grange, we will fall under their political protection in Washington. It seems to me a legal way to protect our farms against Parker and the ranchers. Well, that's my idea. What do you think of it?"

"Will the Grange take my kind?" Mal said.

"I think the Grange is more concerned with what you grow than the color of your skin," James said.

"Then I not only support the idea, I recommend we send James to Minneapolis to talk to them," Mal said.

"Now wait a minute, I wasn't—" James said, but his friends and neighbors shouted him down in agreement with Mal Jones.

Finally James surrendered and quieted the group by waving his hands.

"I'll go and represent us to the Grange," James said. "But I would like to take one more of us to show our support. I also think we should write them first and tell them we're coming."

While all agreed with James, they couldn't agree on who should accompany him. The argument grew so heated that the women entered the barn to see what the fuss was about.

As James sheepishly explained to the women what the discussion was about, the women suggested they put it to a secret vote on who should accompany James to Minneapolis.

Mal Jones won in a landslide.

# NINETEEN

Jason wandered into town shortly after eleven in the evening. He was euphoric on the sweet smell of Amy Uggla's skin and hair that lingered in his nose. Earlier, he rode out and hobbled his horse in some trees a hundred yards or so from the Jones farm, and then walked in behind the house and met Amy after dark behind the Jones's barn.

They watched the fireworks, which went on for twenty minutes or so, and then they snuggled in behind a haystack where, after much playing hard to get, she allowed him to kiss her.

The kissing came to an abrupt halt when they heard the voices of men talking inside the barn. A woman called for Amy. She said it was her ma, and she had to go. She left him alone.

He should have left then, but the conversations inside the barn drew him nearer to the open back window.

After an earful, the women came in and broke things up. Jason walked back to his horse and rode into town guided by a nearly full moon and a well-worn trail.

By the time he reached town, most of the celebrating was over and just a few people remained on the streets. Jason hitched his horse to the post outside the saloon and went in for a cold beer.

John Parker and Teasel were having beers at a table, and they scooted Jason over before he could make it to the bar.

"Mr. Parker wants to see you right away," Teasel said.

78

"Now?" Jason said. "I ain't had my beer yet."

"There's cold ones in a bucket of ice in the hotel room," John said. "Let's go."

Jason was fascinated by the glass bottle full of cold beer that Teasel handed him from an ice bucket. The bottle was sealed with a cork, and when he removed it the beer exploded from the neck of the bottle in creamy foam.

He took a sip of the icy beer. It was delicious, better than from the saloon tap.

John and Teasel grabbed bottles of their own and sat at the table to wait for Parker to arrive.

They didn't wait long. Parker burst through the door before Jason finished half his bottle.

Frightened by the look on Parker's face, Jason jumped up from his chair and spilled some of his beer.

"Mr. Parker," Jason said timidly.

"Were you at the Jones farm tonight?" Parker said.

"I was . . . but no one saw me," Jason said, figuring he would be fired from his job as cowhand. "Except Amy and she won't . . ."

"Sit down, son," Parker said. "I won't bite you. I just want to ask you a few questions."

"Yes, sir," Jason said as he took his chair.

Parker pulled out a long cigar and used a penknife to slice off one end. He lit the cigar with a wood match and then, puffing clouds of gray smoke, took the chair opposite Jason.

"You say no one saw you tonight. Are you sure of that?" Parker said.

"Yes, sir," Jason said. "I mean . . . just Amy . . . she's who I rode out to see. We're kind of sweet on each other, and she won't tell no one or she'd get in trouble."

"What was going on there tonight?" Parker said. "I heard the farmers were celebrating the Fourth all by themselves."

"Yes, sir, that's true," Jason said. "They even had fireworks and everything."

"How is it no one saw you?" Parker said.

"I hobbled my horse down the road and walked in behind the barn after dark and met Amy behind a big haystack," Jason said. "I would have stayed a bit longer 'cept the men had this meeting in the barn, and then Amy's ma called for her."

"Meeting?" Parker said. "Did you hear about what?"

"I couldn't tell who was talking all the time, but someone said the name Johansen," Jason said. "And what they was talking about was sending someone to talk to the Grange back east somewhere. I think they said Minneapolis. They said Johansen should be the one to go and that someone named Jones should go with him."

"Anything else?"

"After that is when the women came in and broke it up," Jason said. "Mr. Parker, am I fired?"

"Fired?" Parker said. "Son, you just got a raise. Head on back to the ranch. There's work tomorrow."

"Yes, sir," Jason said.

After Jason left the room, Parker went to the table where a bottle of brandy and glasses rested. He filled a glass from the bottle.

"Did you hear that? The Grange?" Parker said. "Do you have any idea the political clout the Grange has in Washington?"

"From what I've heard, as much as the Cattlemen's Association," Teasel said.

"That's right, and if they get their hooks into this territory, things could get politically messy for a long time," Parker said.

"Pa, why don't we quit fooling with these farmers and show them who runs things around here?" John said.

"I think I have to agree with John, Mr. Parker," Teasel said.

"And what do you propose?" Parker said. "We shoot it out with the farmers? Burn their homes down, destroy their crops? That is no way to get the attention of Washington as far as statehood goes. We need to be more subtle than that."

"Like how, Pa?" John said.

"Teasel, I want you to ride over to Casper tomorrow and send a telegram for me," Parker said. "Make sure you wait for a reply. I don't care if it takes days. I'll give you hotel and eating money, but you stay and wait for a reply."

"Sure thing, Mr. Parker," Teasel said.

"You boys head back to the ranch," Parker said. "I'm staying in town tonight. Teasel, I'll see you for breakfast and give you the telegram in the morning."

And the telegram read:

*Cord. In dire need of your services. Will discuss details upon your arrival. Jefferson Parker.*

# TWENTY

By the end of the second week of July, the crops were on maintenance, and James had the time to plant a vegetable garden for Sarah at the side of the house. She wanted carrots, green beans, alfalfa, tomatoes and peppers. Once he had the quarter acre in the ground, James and Seth dug an irrigation ditch from the outdoor pump directly to the garden so they could water the patch by simply cranking the pump handle.

On Wednesday of the third week in July, James received a letter from the Grange in Minneapolis. The letter said they would welcome the visit and application to become a member of the Grange.

The following Saturday morning, the group of farmers held a meeting at the Johansen farm. Everyone kicked in, and one hundred dollars was raised to send James and Mal to Minneapolis by train. The money would cover the train tickets, hotel bill and food on the trip.

Plans were made to leave Monday morning. They would ride south to Medicine Bow and catch the train west to Minneapolis. They figured to be gone for ten days. Uggla said he would stop by and check on both families while James and Mal were away.

Mal said he owned no proper traveling clothes, but would purchase some at the general store on Sunday.

The meeting ended when Sarah served hot apple pie and coffee, and milk for the children.

Afterward, James and Sarah sat on the porch with cups of

coffee and James smoked his pipe.

"Once we get the Grange in Minneapolis, I'm sure we can convince the town council to finally build a school and a church," James said.

"Let's not get too far ahead of ourselves," Sarah cautioned. "Mr. Parker is not going to take this news too kindly."

"I don't see where there's much he can do about an official government agency organizing a charter here," James said.

"James, Mr. Parker is not a man to be put off lightly," Sarah said. "He has money, power and men. Don't underestimate what powerful men will do to hold onto their power if they feel threatened."

"I know that, honey," James said. "Just don't go counting me out of the fight before it's even started. I'm pretty tough, you know."

"Tough enough to stop a bullet?"

"Now honey, there hasn't even been any rough stuff, much less gunplay," James said.

Sarah sipped her coffee and looked at the dark clouds brewing in the distance.

James puffed on his pipe as he did when something was on his mind.

"What is it, James?" Sarah said. "Whenever something is on your mind you puff smoke like the Santa Fe."

"I was thinking maybe you should go with us to Minneapolis," James said. "They have this big hospital there and maybe we could see a doctor about . . . having more children."

"James, we are in perfect health. When the times comes for us to have another child, that is when we will have it," Sarah said. "Now come inside and let's pack for your trip. I have to brush off your suit and polish up those old shoes of yours."

James looked at the darkening clouds.

"Storm's coming," he said.

"Yes, it is," Sarah agreed.

# TWENTY-ONE

On Sunday, while James tended to the fields, Sarah and Seth took the wagon to town to buy a can of shoe polish, as the can they had in the house was nearly empty.

When they arrived at Tobey's general store, Mal Jones was in the process of trying on a suit of clothes for the trip east. It was a fine brown suit with a white shirt and thick red tie. The funny-looking hat that Seth had never seen before was called a derby. To Seth it looked like a teakettle sitting on top of Mr. Jones's head.

"It looks fine," Sarah told Mal. "Very handsome."

"I best change," Mal said. "I don't want to get it dirty before the trip."

While Mal went into the back room to change his clothes, Sarah asked Mr. Tobey for the polish and Seth eyed the candy counter. Sarah allowed him one candy stick. Seth went to the door to look out and eat it while Sarah browsed through a catalog on the counter.

Mal came out with his new suit wrapped in brown paper, said good-bye to Sarah and Seth and left the general store.

Mal packed his new suit in the wagon along with the list of possibles Keri wanted. He was about to climb aboard the buckboard when he was suddenly surrounded by six armed men.

One he recognized as John Parker, the rancher's boy. Hard-looking and mean, he held a nine-foot-long leather whip in his

85

right hand, the kind of whip they used on the Georgia plantations.

"You can't speak to no white woman that way, boy," John said.

"What?" Mal said.

"You heard me," John said. He cracked the whip loosely at his side.

"There's no one on the street," Mal said. "I've spoken to no one."

"You calling me a liar?" John said.

"I think he is," the man to Mal's left said. "His kind are all liars and thieves."

Mal saw the look in John's eyes. The man was eager, almost joyful at the notion of inflecting pain.

Mal watched John's right hand and saw the forearm twitch. He knew the crack of the whip was coming.

As John brought his arm high into an arc, Mal dove under his wagon to avoid the whip striking his face and eyes.

The horses spooked and rose up, but the brake was on. That caused them to panic and kick at the wagon with their hind legs.

"Get him out of there!" John shouted.

Mal kicked at the hands that reached for him, but there were too many, and he was pulled on his belly from under the wagon.

"Soften him up," John said.

Two cowboys held Mal by the arms while two others worked him over with fists. After a dozen bone-crushing punches to Mal's face and stomach, he was close to unconscious.

"Get that shirt off him and hold him over the hitching post," John said.

Cowboys started to rip Mal's shirt off. By now a crowd had gathered on the sidewalk and the street. People were screaming at John to stop, but John paid no attention and raised the whip.

Sarah was suddenly in John's face. "You stop this right now!" she screamed.

"Get out of my way, woman," John said.

"Mal Jones never hurt a soul, you piece of filth," Sarah said.

With his left hand, John backhanded Sarah, knocking her to the street. Instantly, Seth was off the porch and attacking John with his tiny fists.

"You hit my ma! You hit my ma!" Seth cried.

John shoved Seth to the street beside Sarah and she immediately covered him with her body.

"You men stop this at once!" Tobey yelled from the porch.

"Somebody get the sheriff," a man hollered.

"Anybody interferes tastes this whip instead of him," John said and arced his right arm high in the air.

And as he yanked the whip forward it snagged on something.

John spun around. That *something* was a tall, dark, lean stranger in black trail clothes and black hat, cradling a thirty-six-inch-barrel Sharps rifle. Low on his gun belt on the right side hung a holstered .44 Smith & Wesson blued revolver. On the left side of his chest in a reverse holster hung a .38 Colt revolver, short-nose special.

"Mister, get your foot off my whip before I use it on you," John said.

"I've seen you hit a woman and a boy. How are you when they come a bit bigger?" the stranger said.

"You mean you?" John said.

"Having any?"

John looked at the way the stranger held the massive rifle in both arms at the elbows, dropped the whip and reached for his .45 Colt.

The stranger hardly seemed to move at all, but the rifle was suddenly in his left hand and the Smith & Wesson .44 was out and cocked before John cleared his holster.

"Now that wasn't very nice, drawing on me," the stranger said as he walked to John. "In fact, that was downright rude behavior."

The stranger uncocked the .44 and then smashed John in the jaw with it. John was out before he hit the street.

Before any of the cowboys could move, the stranger holstered the .44 and aimed the Sharps rifle at the two men holding Mal over the hitching post.

"Ma, did you see . . . ?" Seth said.

"Quiet, Seth," Sarah said.

The stranger slowly walked to the two cowboys at the post.

"This town got a doctor?" the stranger said.

"Got a barber who does some doctoring," one of the cowboys said.

"You two take this man to see the barber," the stranger said. "Whatever he charges for his doctoring, that man pays the bill."

The stranger pointed the Sharps rifle at John.

The cowboys nodded.

"Go," the stranger said.

"Give us a hand," the two cowboys said and the other cowboys helped lift Mal and carry him across the street to the barbershop.

The stranger turned without so much as a glance backward and walked to his massive brown stallion, mounted him and rode down the street.

"Ma, did you see . . . ?" Seth said.

Sarah grabbed Seth's hand and yanked him to the sidewalk and rushed down the street to an alleyway.

"Ma, we have to thank . . . ," Seth said.

"Be quiet Seth and listen to me," Sarah said. "Your father must never know about this. Ever."

"Ma, that man . . ."

"Seth, be quiet and understand what I'm telling you," Sarah

said. "If your pa finds out that John Parker struck you and me, he will ride out to the Parker Ranch and want to avenge us. Your pa is no gunfighter. He'll want to use fists, and they will shoot him down like a rabid dog. Do you understand?"

"I understand, Ma," Seth said.

"Promise me you will never tell your father what happened."

"I promise."

"Come on. We have to tell Mr. Tobey never to speak of this to your father."

Sarah led Seth by the hand back to the general store and had him wait on the sidewalk while she went in to see Mr. Tobey.

The crowd around Seth buzzed with excitement, and some said John Parker got exactly what he deserved from the stranger.

Seth looked up and down the street for the stranger, but there was no sign of him anywhere. It was as if he was never there.

Then Ma came out and took him by the hand. "Let's go home," she said.

## TWENTY-TWO

"I can't say as I am at all pleased with my son's behavior, Mr. Cord," Parker said.

Cord and Parker were in the den at the ranch house. Parker sat behind his massive, highly polished oak desk. Cord took one of the padded, comfortable chairs facing the desk.

Both men had small snifters of brandy.

Parker smoked a cigar. He offered one to Cord, but the man refused.

Instead he rolled a cigarette from a well-worn pouch of tobacco.

"I didn't know he was your son at the time, but had I known, I would have done the same," Cord said.

"My son doesn't always use good judgment," Parker said. "The sore jaw he's nursing will help him make better decisions in the future."

Cord sipped from his snifter and then inhaled on the cigarette. "All right, Mr. Parker, let's get to it," he said. "You sent for me because?"

"Wyoming is cattle country, Mr. Cord," Parker said. "Wide open ranges from the Black Hills to the Eastern Rockies, the way God intended it to be. We're looking at statehood inside a decade. The problem is the influx of farmers moving in, closing off the land to grow their potatoes and corn. Enough of them move in, and the cattle have less and less range. Pretty soon there will be none at all. Now the railroad in Medicine Bow doesn't service cattle. We need the Santa Fe to build tracks to move our stock to market. None of this will happen if the farms close off the land."

"You want to drive the farmers out, is that it?" Cord said.

"They have formed some kind of committee and are sending a representative to Minneapolis to talk to the Grange," Parker said. "If they are given a charter, more and more farmers will come from the east, and our open ranges will close off."

"Let me guess. That man your son was about to whip, it wasn't because of the color of his skin," Cord said.

"Malachi Jones has one hundred and sixty acres three hours south of town," Parker said. "He and James Johansen were selected to go to Minneapolis to the Grange."

"And your son thought whipping him would do what to help your cause?" Cord said.

"Like I said, my son's judgment isn't always the best," Parker said. "Johansen is the real leader of the bunch. The others follow his lead. Now I'm not asking for gunplay, not at this point. I'm willing to buy out each farm for cash money. I need someone to speak to the farmers on my behalf and persuade them that selling is in their best interest, so to speak."

"What are you offering?" Cord said.

"The average farm brings in about three hundred a year at harvest," Parker said. "Three hundred per farm is my offer."

"Mr. Parker, it is obvious you know a great deal about cattle, but you know shit about people," Cord said. "A man works like a dog to raise the money to buy his land, and then he breaks his back working the land to grow his crops, he isn't going to sell for a year's worth of harvest. More than likely all you'll do is start a range war and cause bloodshed."

"What do you suggest?" Parker said.

"Twelve hundred per farm is a fair offer," Cord said. "A man could buy a new farm somewhere else and have a few years' worth of savings in the bank while he starts over."

"That's almost seventeen thousand dollars you're talking about."

"How much is that land worth to your cattle, the railroad and statehood?" Cord said. " 'Course I'm only guessing here, but I see you making a run as first governor when Wyoming is admitted to the Union."

Parker had to smile at Cord's brashness and an intelligence he hadn't expected in so feared a hired gunman. "Say I agree to twelve hundred per farm, how will you approach the farmers with the offer?"

"Ask them," Cord said.

"And if they refuse?"

"I'll explain to them the dire need they have to sell," Cord said.

Parker allowed himself a soft chuckle. "Let's talk about your fee."

"My fee is what I say it is and is not negotiable," Cord said.

"And that would be what?"

"One hundred head prime from your herd, and expense money for as long as the job takes to complete," Cord said.

"A hundred head?" Parker said. "Whatever for?"

"I have three thousand acres in California," Cord said. "When my herd is large enough, I plan to retire there. My expense money will be one hundred a week. I work alone, and it would be in your best interest to keep your men on your ranch during the week. If they must go to town on Saturday to do their drinking and whoring, tell them to leave their guns in the bunkhouse. Under no circumstances are they to interfere with me in any way. Starting with your son."

Parker nodded. "Don't worry about John. I want him nowhere near this."

"Have you a trusted man above the others?"

"My foreman Teasel."

"Where is he?"

"On the range, I expect."

"Due back?"

"Late this afternoon, I expect."

"I'll be at the hotel in town," Cord said. "Have him ride out to see me."

"What for?"

"After today I won't be back to your ranch until the job is complete," Cord said. "He will act as my liaison to you if and when we need to communicate."

"Teasel is a ranch foreman, not a messenger," Parker said. "He won't like that."

Cord stood up, squashed out the cigarette in a crystal ashtray, tossed back what was left in the brandy snifter and looked at Parker.

"That wasn't a request," Cord said.

# TWENTY-THREE

"I'm sorry, James, but I won't be fit to travel for at least a week," Mal said from his bed.

"Sarah said you have a concussion," James said. "Our trip can wait a week or so while you mend."

"That Parker boy is evil, James," Mal said. "Not slick like his daddy, but mean."

"If we had a real sheriff, he'd be behind bars waiting trial for assault," James said.

"I didn't see much of it. I was out mostly, but that stranger who stopped the Parker boy," Mal said. "I never got to say a proper thank-you."

"I heard what he done," James said. "I'll ask around town and see if anyone knows him. Maybe he's still around."

"James, listen to me now," Mal said. "Don't wait on me. Them people at the Grange is expecting us to see them, and being late is a real bad start. You don't need nobody with you to talk on our behalf. You know what to say. Don't wait. Go."

"We'll talk about it when you're feeling better," James said.

"By then it be too late," Mal said. "Everybody is counting on you, James. Don't let us down."

"I hear the Overland Stage is coming through in two days and going on to Medicine Bow after that," James said. "I could save a few days in the saddle and grab the train east from there."

"Do it, James," Mal said. "Now go fetch Keri and ask her to come in and bring me some of that medicine for my headache."

"All right, and then you get some rest," James said.

"I think it's a fine idea taking the stage to Medicine Bow, but I wish you would ask another man to go with you," Sarah said.

"I can take care of myself," James said. "I'll explain to the Grange what happened to Mal. That should serve to show them how important it is for them to grant us membership."

"I guess there is no sense trying to talk you out of this," Sarah said. "I'll go dust off your suit and give your shoes a fresh coat of polish."

James spent the rest of the afternoon and into the early evening chopping wood to ensure Sarah had an adequate supply while he was away.

Seth finished his chores and sat to watch his father swing the ax.

"Pa, how long you figure to be gone?" Seth said.

James swung the heavy ax through a thick log and it split into two parts. "A day's ride on the stage. Overnight at the hotel, and two days to Minneapolis on the train. A day to talk to the Grange, and then I'll head back. A week or eight days should do it."

"What if something needs tending I can't handle?" Seth said.

"Like what?"

"Something, I don't know."

James set another log on the block. "Don't sell your ma short," he said as he swung the ax and split the log. "She can handle the team and chop wood as well as any man. As long as you keep up your chores, everything should be fine until I get back."

"Yes, Pa," Seth said.

"Speaking of chores, isn't it about time our cow was ready to donate another bucket of milk?" James said.

"I almost forgot," Seth said as he ran off to the barn.

Just before he fell asleep, Sarah shook James awake.

"James, listen to me for a moment," Sarah said.

"I was asleep, hon," James said.

"I have to take the wagon into town in the morning," Sarah said. "I'm very low on baking supplies, and I want to stock up before you go. I'll pick up your ticket to the stage and save you a bit of time."

"That's good, hon," James said. "I can use the time to check the fields."

A moment later James was asleep and Sarah rested her head on his chest and held her husband tight as if she were afraid to let him go. She closed her eyes, but the images of John Parker, Mal and the stranger kept flashing through her mind. Once she felt James was sound asleep, Sarah slipped out of bed and quietly went to the tiny icebox in the kitchen and filled a glass with cold milk.

She took the milk out to the porch and sat in a chair. The nearly full moon was bright enough to almost read by. She sipped the milk and listened to the sound of night.

Crickets and peepers.

An owl and a frog.

Chickens restlessly sleeping in the coop.

A soft breeze blowing in from the south.

And suddenly the stray cat was on the porch and meowing for a sip of the milk. The empty saucer was beside her chair so Sarah poured a bit of milk onto it, and the cat went right to work lapping it up.

Sarah sat and felt the breeze on her face and wondered if the farm, this patch of land and field, was worth the trouble she knew was on its way.

# Twenty-Four

Cord was having breakfast in the hotel dining room when Teasel came in and nodded to the waitress for coffee before joining Cord at his table.

"Mr. Parker told me to meet you here," Teasel said.

The waitress brought Teasel a full cup of coffee and set it on the table.

"And he told me you're a top foreman and a man who can be trusted," Cord said.

"That is what I am," Teasel said. "What I ain't is a messenger boy."

"I know that," Cord said. "I dislike towns. For as long as this job takes I'll set up camp about two miles to the east. I saw a creek there and I like to have fresh water nearby. All I'm asking from you is to keep Parker's hothead son on a leash and carry word to Parker when I need it. I'll try to solve this situation without any more blood spilled. I have the feeling the Parker boy holds the opposite view."

Teasel sipped from his cup. "Why does a hired gun care if blood is spilled or not?" he said.

Cord, eating steak and eggs, sliced off a piece of steak, put it in his mouth and slowly chewed. "Because there is always the chance that some of the blood spilled might belong to me," he said. "And because I don't want to have to kill the son of my employer."

Teasel nodded. "Fair enough," he said. "Although John goes

97

his own way and doesn't always show the best judgment about things."

"That's where you keep him out of it," Cord said. "Don't give him the chance to make poor decisions."

"And if he won't listen?" Teasel said.

Cord set down his knife and fork, sipped coffee from his cup and then set that aside. "If I have to kill that boy because of your failure, I will kill you next for your failure," he said.

Cord made his threat with such ease and with no more regard for the word kill he might have been ordering more coffee.

Teasel felt a chill run down his back. In his forty years he had seen many a mean, backstabbing cutthroat and bushwhacker, but the genuine articles were few and very far between.

Cord was the genuine article.

Of that Teasel had no doubt.

"I'll speak to Mr. Parker," Teasel said. "Maybe I can convince him to keep John on the range with me until this is done."

"That would be wise," Cord said. "After you talk to Parker, come see me at my camp. We'll break bread. And if anybody else but you shows up at my camp, you will never hear the bullet that kills you."

Cord rode out of town with his horse loaded down with supplies and traveled two miles due east to the flowing creek where he pitched his lean-to on the bank. He had enough supplies for ten days. If the job ran longer, it was a short ride to restock.

After setting up the lean-to, Cord broke down his supplies and placed canned goods, coffee, beans, bacon and salt into a large sack, tied a rope around it and hung it from the branch of a tall tree where animals wouldn't be able to get to it. He had six bottles of beer and he placed them into another sack, tied a rope around it and then tied it to a tree near the creek and tossed it into the cool water to keep the beer cold.

Then he built a fire to make a pot of coffee and went about the task of cleaning his weapons.

He started with the Sharps rifle and used his small tool kit designed for taking apart weapons to strip the massive rifle right down to the trigger spring. He used wire brushes, cleaning cloths and oil on the many parts, then carefully assembled the rifle back into one piece.

He repeated the procedure on his Winchester 73 model rifle, .44 Smith & Wesson and the short-nose special.

After he was satisfied all were cleaned, oiled, loaded and in excellent working condition, Cord withdrew the knife from its sheath on the left side of his gun belt. It was an army regulation bayonet, fourteen inches of razor-sharp edge and blued to a dark finish. It was the sharpest, most reliable knife he had ever owned. Using a smooth stone he kept for just such a purpose, he put an edge on the bayonet that would shave chin whiskers.

Slowly the sun shifted across the sky. By late afternoon Cord decided to take a nap inside the lean-to. He brought the Sharps, Winchester and gun belt in with him and was asleep within seconds.

Sarah rode the wagon into town alone, as Seth had his chores and James went to the fields to do a final check on the crops before he left for Medicine Bow in the morning.

Tickets for the Overland Stage were sold in the general store. The price for a round-trip ticket was twelve dollars, fifty cents extra for baggage that needed to be stored on top.

As she left the general store with the ticket, Sarah stopped dead in her tracks on the sidewalk when she saw the stranger exit the hotel across the street and walk directly toward her.

She stepped down to the wagon and turned her face away from his as the stranger passed, climbed up the steps and entered the store.

When he was inside the store, Sarah knew the thing to do was ride on back home, but something held her back. She looked up and down the street, but what few people who were about paid her no mind.

Sarah slowly took the three wood steps up to the sidewalk, stood outside the general store and looked over the swinging doors. The stranger was at the counter, and Mr. Tobey was reading from a list of supplies.

Sarah pushed in the swinging doors as quietly as possible and slowly walked up behind the stranger. He was tall, at least a half a foot taller than James, and James was not a short man. His shoulders were wide as a barn door yet his hips were slim. He placed his hands on the counter. They were massive hands with swollen knuckles.

Then he said, "I'll be back in an hour to pick everything up," and turned so quickly he nearly bumped into Sarah.

She looked at his face and into his eyes. His beard was speckled with gray, as was his shoulder-length hair under his hat. His eyes were gray and seemed to lack life, like the way the eyes of a snake didn't seem alive or even real. Mostly they were hypnotic.

He touched his hat with his right finger and then stepped around her and left the store. He showed no sign of recognizing her from that other, awful violent day.

"Sarah?" Mr. Tobey said. "Did you forget something?"

"Yes," Sarah said. "I would like ten cents' worth of penny candy for Seth."

A minute later when Sarah left the store, the stranger was nowhere to be seen. She boarded the wagon and then realized she was breathless and her skin felt warm, as if she had been blushing.

And she didn't know why.

★ ★ ★ ★ ★

When Cord opened his eyes from his nap, he saw, in his mind, the face of the dark-haired woman in the general store.

And he didn't know why.

# TWENTY-FIVE

"For God's sake, Pa, we don't need some hired gun to beat a bunch of stupid farmers," John said. "Let me take some of the boys and . . ."

"For the last time, John, you listen to me," Parker said. "This is not about beating some stupid farmers, as you say. This is about statehood and political power and the very future of our livelihood. I want you to stay on the ranch and work the range with Teasel until this business is finished. You are not to go to town or bother one single farmer. Am I clear?"

John, standing before his father's desk, stared at Parker.

"Am I clear?" Parker said.

"Yes," John hissed through clenched teeth.

"Now go earn your keep," Parker said. "I expect every man who works for me to pull his own weight, and that includes you, son or no son."

John glared at Parker and then turned and stomped out of the den.

Seated in a chair opposite the desk, Teasel sighed openly. "He's none too happy, Mr. Parker."

"My son is young and he is foolish," Parker said. "I want you to work him sunup to sundown and make sure he is too tired to go off to town at night. Now go see Cord and tell him my son won't be a bother. Then ask him what his plans are for dealing with these farmers."

"Yes, sir, Mr. Parker," Teasel said and stood up.

"And make sure John is working the range before you go see Cord."

"There's some strays need rounding up on the east range," Teasel said. "I'll send him and some of the boys. That should take the rest of the day."

"Good."

Teasel found John outside the bunkhouse talking to a few of the men.

"You men got nothing to do?" Teasel said.

"We just brought in six stray horses from the north range," one of the men said. "Must have got out of the reserve corral."

"Mount up some fresh horses and head out to the east range," Teasel said. "Some strays wandered from the herd. Take supplies for overnight in case you don't make it back by nightfall."

"Sure thing," the man said.

"You go with them, John," Teasel said.

"I don't take orders from you," John said.

"That order ain't from me," Teasel said. "And if you don't like it, you can go argue the point with Mr. Parker. Get a fresh horse and join these men in the east range."

Teasel turned away from John and walked toward his horse, mounted up and rode away.

"Now where's he going?" John said.

"Never mind where he's going," a man said. "We got work to do."

Teasel approached the creek with caution. He didn't want to spook Cord into shooting him at long range the way he knew the man was capable of doing.

He rode along the embankment for a mile or so and spotted a lean-to a few hundred yards up ahead. The last fifty yards he dismounted and walked his horse into Cord's camp.

Cord appeared to have set up camp for an extended stay.

"Cord, it's Teasel!" he shouted.

Teasel waited. Slowly Cord stood up from where he was hiding along the embankment of the creek. He had the massive Sharps rifle in his arms.

"No need for that," Teasel said.

"If there were, I would have shot you a thousand yards out," Cord said. "Coffee is still hot. Want a cup?"

"Sure."

Cord filled two tin mugs and they sat against a tree facing the creek. Cord rolled a cigarette and gave it to Teasel and then rolled another for himself. He struck a match and lit both.

"Mr. Parker is going to keep his son working the range until you've finished your business," Teasel said.

"Will his son listen?"

"Honestly, I don't know. The boy is young and full of juice and a hothead to boot," Teasel said.

"Make him listen."

Teasel nodded. "Mr. Parker asked me what your plans are."

"I'm going to visit each farm and relay Parker's offer and give them time to think it over," Cord said. "I figure they'll wait until Johansen returns from the Grange and then they'll have a meeting. I'll attend that meeting. After that I'll be able to tell Parker what the situation looks like, and he can decide the next course of action he wants to take. Parker wants a peaceful solution to this problem, and I aim to give it to him."

"I'll tell him that."

"Do you know the locations of these farms?"

"One or two of them."

"Can you find out?" Cord said. "Deeds must be on record in town, maybe at the bank?"

"I'll see what I can do," Teasel said. "I can tell you directions to the Johansen place, Uggla and Jones. Jones is the black fellow you saved from a whipping."

"That's a start," Cord said. "Check at the bank and let me know in the next few days. If I'm not here, leave me a note."

Less than a mile from the east range, John broke away from the other cowboys, backtracked and picked up Teasel's trail.

The man was headed for the creek that came down from the East Rockies and flowed along the hills to the valley. Why was he going there? Maybe he had a woman stashed away somewhere?

John followed the trail of Teasel's tracks until, about a thousand yards or so ahead he spotted something. He pulled the binoculars from his saddlebags and zoomed in on Teasel and Cord having coffee against a tree.

"I guess I best head back and see Mr. Parker," Teasel said.

"Hold on a second," Cord said.

Teasel watched as Cord stood up and held the Sharps rifle in his arms and aimed at something. He lowered the rifle and adjusted the sights a few clicks and then aimed again.

Teasel stood up.

"What are you . . . ?" Teasel said just as Cord fired.

A thousand yards away the bullet struck the ground at a horse's legs, and the spooked horse reared up and threw its rider.

Cord lowered the Sharps and looked at Teasel.

"Now you ride out and tell that stupid Parker boy that I didn't have to miss," Cord said.

John was bleeding from a cut on his forehead and had a few bruises on his cheeks from the fall off his horse when Teasel rode out and found him still on the ground.

"Are you getting up or taking a nap?" Teasel said.

"Had the wind knocked out of me," John said.

"Maybe so, but he could have put one between your eyes if he'd had a mind to," Teasel said. "What did you follow me for, anyway? I told you to work the strays."

"I got curious."

"Now you know, and you best stay away from that man if you know what's good for you," Teasel said.

John got up and mounted his horse. "He don't scare me none."

"Don't you recognize a rattlesnake when you see one?" Teasel said. "Now let's get back to the ranch. I'll tell Mr. Parker you fell roping a stray."

There wasn't enough daylight to burn riding out to the closest farms, so Cord broke camp and moved it about a mile on the other side of the creek.

If that Parker boy returned looking for some payback, he wouldn't find any.

Come morning he'd get an early start and ride out to the Johansen, Jones and Uggla farms and start negotiations.

# TWENTY-SIX

James drove the wagon to town and parked it in front of Tobey's store to wait for the Overland Stage to arrive at noon or so. Sarah sat beside him. Once he was off, she would drive the wagon home.

While James chatted up a storm of excitement about the upcoming trip, Sarah kept a cautious eye on the streets for signs of trouble. By trouble, she meant the Parker boy and other hands from Parker's ranch.

Thankfully none were about.

Luckily the stage arrived a few minutes early.

"Why don't you go on home, hon?" James said. "It won't take them but a few minutes to change out the horses."

"I'll wait and see you off," Sarah said.

"The boy is alone."

"With chores to do that better be finished when I get back."

The Overland driver walked a fresh team to the stagecoach and hooked the six horses into place.

"I best be off," James said and kissed Sarah lightly on the lips.

Sarah watched James carry his suitcase onto the stage with him, and after a few other passengers joined him, the driver and security guard climbed aboard. They rode quickly down Main Street and out of town.

Sarah released the brake handle, jiggled the reins, and slowly rode the wagon in the opposite direction toward home.

Cord tied a white pillowcase to the barrel of the Sharps rifle before riding into the Uggla farm.

A woman of about forty whom he took for Uggla's wife was working a hoe in a small garden in front of the farmhouse. A corral contained two horses. Some chickens pecked around. Behind the house to the left stood a barn painted red. The sun had faded the color.

On the porch of the house a girl of about fifteen whom he took for the daughter of the woman in the garden churned butter.

Mother and daughter stopped what they were doing and looked at Cord as he slowly rode onto their property.

The mother dropped the hoe, walked to the corral and picked up a double-barrel shotgun and held it loosely aimed at Cord.

"You won't need that," Cord said.

"I'll judge that," the woman said. "What do you want?"

"Speak with you and your family on behalf of Jefferson Parker," Cord said.

"Amy, fetch your father from the barn."

After Amy served sweet lemonade, Uggla and his wife and Cord sat on the porch to talk. Amy was told to go inside, but she listened from the open window that overlooked the front yard.

"Twelve hundred dollars is a great deal of money," Uggla said. "Parker must want this land pretty bad to make such an offer."

"Cattle require a great deal of land, and he's afraid if enough people move in and take up farming, there won't be enough to raise a herd," Cord said.

"He's making that offer to everyone?" Uggla said.

"Every farmer inside the county," Cord said.

"That's a lot of money."

"Parker has a lot of money," Cord said.

"And what's your stake in this?" Uggla said.

"Parker hired me to negotiate his terms with you farmers."

"You're a hired gun," Uggla said. "Isn't that about the size of it?"

"Mr. Uggla, let me explain something to you," Cord said. "I've seen this kind of situation before. Many times it leads to bloodshed. I aim to prevent that if I can. Twelve hundred is three times what your farm is worth, and we both know it. If you took the offer, you could relocate elsewhere, buy new land and still have quite a bit left in the bank."

"And if I refuse?" Uggla said.

"I'm sure Parker's deal is all inclusive," Cord said.

"Mr. . . . ?" Mrs. Uggla said.

"Cord."

"Mr. Cord, you sound like a very intelligent man," Mrs. Uggla said. "Please don't assume that because we are farmers that we are stupid."

"There's no call for that kind of talk," Uggla said to his wife.

"No, let her say what's on her mind," Cord said. "It's not speaking your mind that leads to bloodshed."

"We left our farm in Minnesota when three years of hard winter destroyed our fields," Mrs. Uggla said. "We traveled a thousand miles in a covered wagon and spent our entire life savings to buy this land. That was five years ago. The first two years we lost money. The third year we broke even. Last year we made a profit of nearly three hundred dollars. You're asking us to pack up and move away from a place we know will turn a profit in the future for something unknown somewhere else. How much is that kind of risk worth to you?"

Cord nodded. "You want more money?"

"Five thousand plus expenses for moving."

"Parker will never go for . . . ," Uggla said.

"Then we stay put," Mrs. Uggla said. "I will not spend three months in a covered wagon again, not at my age, not with Amy a budding woman and not for such a high risk. You tell Parker those are our terms."

"I'll tell him," Cord said.

Cord stood and walked off the porch to his horse. Uggla followed him.

"My wife is . . . well, she does have a point," Uggla said. "We have roots here now. It will be hard to move and start over."

"Your friend who went to the Grange," Cord said. "I suggest you wait until he returns with news and then hold a meeting to discuss terms."

"Terms?" Uggla said. "You sound very sure of how this will turn out."

"I know how it will turn out," Cord said. "I hope you're on the right side."

"If there's shooting?" Uggla said.

"If you raise a gun to me, I will kill you," Cord said.

Uggla looked up at Cord. The man was six or seven inches taller than he, and the man's stone-cold gray eyes sent a chill running down his back.

Cord mounted his horse.

"Think over what I said," Cord said. "I'll tell Parker your terms."

"Are you the man who helped my husband?" Keri Jones said to Cord when he rode up showing the white pillowcase on the end of the Sharps rifle.

"Yes," Cord said as he dismounted.

Behind Keri, her son Cal hugged her tight around the waist.

"Is that your boy hiding there?" Cord said.

110

"My son Calvin," Keri said.

Cord touched the brim of his hat. "They call you Cal?"

"Yes, sir," Cal said.

Cord looked at Keri. She was a pretty woman, a bit worn from farm life, with smooth brown skin and light-brown eyes. "Is your husband around?"

"I'll get him," Keri said.

"I'm forty-three years old," Mal said. "I've been a free man less than half my life."

Keri served coffee and a crumb cake that Cord thought delicious. Cal had a glass of milk and dipped a piece of cake into the glass and ate it while keeping his eyes locked on Cord.

Cord sipped coffee and looked out over the Jones front yard. The view from the porch told him everything he needed to know about Mal Jones and his family. The corral was in excellent condition, with two fine horses inside it that were well-kept. A small vegetable garden was meticulously cared for, and rows of flowers were growing in several places to add color to the land.

Mal Jones took fierce pride in his home and property.

"I broke my back picking cotton in Georgia almost before I could walk," Mal said. He turned to look at Cal. "Isn't it time you got to milking the old gal?"

"Now?" Cal said.

"You want to wait until she blows an udder?"

"No, sir," Cal said.

Cal stepped down off the porch and went around back to the barn.

Mal looked Cord in the eye after Cal was gone. "My wife, she never worked a day in the fields," he said. "Do you know why?"

Keri lowered her eyes. "Mal, please," she said.

111

"She was born pretty," Mal said. "And when she came of age, she was set aside for pleasuring the master and his staff."

"Mr. Jones, there is no need for me to know those details," Cord said.

"I think you should know why a man gives the answer he gives," Mal said. "We came here a few years ago not knowing what to expect from the people and the land. Some didn't want our kind in town, but our neighbors came from all over and had the same fears we did. After a time, our color no longer mattered. Now I break my back twice as hard as I did on the plantation, but I do it because I want to and not because I have to. This is our land and Mr. Parker can't have it at any price. You tell him the days of buying and selling people are over."

"I appreciate your words, Mr. Jones," Cord said. "But understand this. Men like Parker don't care about the color of your skin or where you're from. They are interested in only one thing, and that's their own power. If they can't buy what they want, they will find a way to take it."

"Then he'll have to take it," Mal said.

"Blood will be spilled," Cord said.

"I bled before," Mal said. "I'm sure I will again."

"I advised the Ugglas to wait for Mr. Johansen to return from the Grange and hold a meeting," Cord said. "I will attend the meeting as Parker's representative and take back to him whatever the final decision is."

"And if the answer is no?" Mal said.

"Then I will advise all to get ready for the fight that will be coming," Cord said.

"I am grateful to you for what you did for me," Mal said. "But if fighting starts and you're with them, I will fight you."

Cord nodded. "I know," he said. He looked at Keri. "The cake was wonderful."

"Ma, somebody is coming!" Seth cried. He dropped the pan of chicken feed and raced up the porch steps. "Ma, there's a man coming!"

Sarah stepped out onto the porch wiping her hands on the apron around her waist.

"Stay on the porch," she said.

"Ma, it's the . . . ," Seth said.

"Stay on the porch," Sarah said and went inside.

Cord, holding the Sharps rifle with white pillowcase in the air, rode in and stopped at the hitching post beside the corral.

Sarah came back out holding James's Navy Colt pistol in her hands. She aimed it at Cord.

"That's far enough," Sarah said.

"Is that a Navy Colt?" Cord said. "I haven't seen one of those in fifteen years. Does it still work?"

"Keep walking and find out," Sarah said.

"If it still works and if you loaded powder, ball and cap properly, seventy-five feet is one hell of a good shot," Cord said. "Have you ever fired that thing? Loaded improperly they tend to blow up in your hand and take your fingers off at the knuckle."

Sarah looked at Cord. The man was so sure of himself that she suddenly felt foolish holding the pistol on him.

"No," she said. "I've never loaded or fired it before."

"Then let's not start losing fingers now."

Sarah lowered the pistol. "What is it you want?"

"Talk," Cord said. "I know your husband is away, but I figure you can tell him when he comes back."

"I just made a pot of coffee," Sarah said. "Come up and take a seat. Seth, run in and bring out cups."

113

★ ★ ★ ★ ★

"I'm afraid my husband would never agree to Mr. Parker's demands," Sarah said.

Cord looked at her and Seth, who was seated to her right.

Sarah felt as if his gray eyes looked right through her and felt almost as if he could read her mind.

"I saw you in the general store the other day," Cord said.

"I was buying my husband's stage ticket," Sarah said.

"Before that?"

"I was there that day you stopped Mal Jones from being whipped."

"I remember. The Parker boy slapped you."

"And me," Seth added.

"Mr. Cord, my husband is no gun hand," Sarah said. "I haven't told him about that day because he will want revenge, and they will kill him. I don't want to see my husband killed over a slap in the face."

"I understand that," Cord said.

"Are you a gunfighter?" Seth said.

"Seth, please be quiet," Sarah said.

"It's all right," Cord said. "Seth, is it? I am a man who solves problems."

"You look like a gunfighter," Seth said.

"Maybe so," Cord said.

"As I said, my husband would never agree to sell to Mr. Parker," Sarah said. "So I'm afraid there is nothing left to say until James returns."

"I advised the others to wait for his return with news from the Grange and then to hold a meeting," Cord said. "I'll attend, and we can discuss Parker's offer at that time."

"I already know what James will say," Sarah said.

"What will he say if there's a threat of bloodshed and his family is in the way?"

"Is that a threat?"

"No," Cord said. "But you know Parker, and you know how he will take the news if his offer is rejected."

"Five thousand dollars is a lot of money."

"Yes, it is."

"Will Parker go that high?"

"He will."

"Then when James returns you tell him and the others," Sarah said.

"That's what I plan to do," Cord said.

Sarah nodded.

Cord looked at her.

She felt her cheeks flush like a schoolgirl.

"Is that Sara, like in Britain, or with an H, like in the Bible?" Cord said.

"H," Sarah said. She knew she was blushing, but she couldn't stop it from happening.

Cord nodded. "I figure your husband will be back in six days," he said. "I'll talk to him when they hold that meeting."

Sarah nodded.

Cord stood and extended his right hand to Seth. The boy took it. His hand all but vanished inside Cord's.

"Take care of your ma while your pa is away," Cord said.

"Yes, sir."

Cord released Seth and extended his hand to Sarah.

Sarah stood up and placed her right hand into Cord's. He shook gently, but she could feel the brute power in his fingers that she knew could crush her bones if he had a mind to.

"Hope to see you again," Cord said. "Sarah with an H."

Sarah had to look away, feeling her neck blush again and feeling as he could look right into her chest and see her rapidly beating heart.

Cord released Sarah's hand and walked down the porch steps

to his horse, mounted up and slowly rode away the way that he came as if he didn't have a care in the world.

Seth looked at his mother.

"Ma, are you all right?" he said. "You look like you have a fever."

"I'm just warm from baking and sitting in the sun," Sarah said. "Go finish your chores. I'm making apple pie for tonight."

"Okay, Ma," Seth said and jumped off the porch. He returned to the chickens and picked up the pan.

He looked into the distance. Mr. Cord was a small black dot on the road.

And Ma was still on the porch watching him ride away.

# Twenty-Seven

Teasel tracked Cord to his new camp and took the liberty of brewing a pot of coffee while he waited for the man to return.

Close to sundown Cord rode in and dismounted by lifting his right leg over the saddle and sliding off in one quick motion.

"Thought you might like some coffee?" Teasel said.

"I do. Thanks."

Cord removed the saddle from his horse and tossed it beside the fire. Then he filled a cup, sat with his back against the saddle and rolled a cigarette.

"Those farmers aren't going to go easy," Cord said.

"I didn't think they would."

"The Uggla woman pulled a shotgun on me, and Sarah Johansen had an old Navy Colt she got from somewhere," Cord said.

Teasel grinned. "Women will fight to the death to protect their cubs," he said.

"Let's hope it don't come to that," Cord said.

"I got basic directions to the other farms," Teasel said and pulled a folded paper from his shirt pocket. "You shouldn't have any trouble finding them."

Cord struck a match on his boot and lit the cigarette. "Let me ask you something," he said. "We both know how the farmers are going to side up, and the same goes for Parker. When the shooting starts, where do you line up?"

"I've worked for Mr. Parker going on ten years," Teasel said.

"I started as a hand, worked my way up to trail boss and now ranch foreman. I owe him a lot."

"Do you owe him murdering farmers and their families?" Cord said.

Teasel looked at Cord.

"If you wind up on the wrong side of things, that's what will happen," Cord said.

"What about you?" Teasel said.

"I got no problem killing," Cord said. "Never have."

The words made Teasel's blood run cold.

"Just make sure when the killing starts you're killing those that deserve it," Cord said.

"I need to head back," Teasel said. "Any message for Mr. Parker?"

"Tell him by the week's end I'll have seen every farmer," Cord said. "I'll come see him in his office in town then."

"I'll tell him," Teasel said.

After Teasel was well out of sight, Cord broke a long branch off a tree, whittled it clean with the bayonet and dug out the fishing line and hooks he kept in his saddlebags. He cut off a strip of line about twelve feet long, tied it to the newly formed pole and tied a hook to the other end of the line.

For bait he cut up some jerked beef and stuck it on the hook. Then he stuck one end on the pole a foot into the dirt along the embankment of the creek and tossed in the line.

He rolled a cigarette, filled his cup with still-hot coffee and sat against a tree to watch the line. Fish were most active at dawn and dusk, so maybe he'd catch a few for supper.

He occupied his thoughts with details of the job. He knew how the farmers would stack up against Parker's offer to buy them out, and he didn't blame them one bit. One man telling another man how to make a living and where he could live wasn't something that would sit well with most men, especially family men who broke their backs to get a little something out of life.

The question in Cord's mind was what would Parker do about rejection? He knew the answer to that question, too. When men like Parker can't buy or bully what they want, they take by force.

In this case, with so much riding on the farmers vacating, how far would Parker push things?

An all-out range war with the farmers?

The farmers wouldn't stand a chance.

Neither would Parker's dream of statehood and a governorship if things got so bad the federal government had to step in to calm things down.

No, Parker was too smart for that kind of play. He would be discreet in the way he would go about driving out the farmers one by one until none remained and he could buy up all the land.

Parker would work on one family at a time; destroy their crops in the dead of night, burn down their houses when they were working the fields, but one way or another Parker would get what he wanted.

The pole suddenly jerked and Cord grabbed it, stood up and yanked hard on the line. He caught a nice one-pound whitefish, removed it from the hook and tossed it on the grass. One more like that, and he'd have supper.

Cord stuck another piece of jerked beef on the hook and tossed in the line. He sat back, rolled another cigarette and waited.

The Parker boy concerned him. If ever Cord saw a man begging to be killed, it was John Parker.

Cord hoped he wouldn't have to be the one to kill the young idiot. Even if it were done in self-defense to protect his own life,

Parker would not stand for his only son and heir being gunned down.

Maybe Teasel could do as he said and keep the hothead confined to the ranch?

Maybe, but doubtful.

Cord had seen too many men in his lifetime who were exactly like the Parker boy. They held the belief that somehow they were immune to a bullet, and they always discovered too late that they weren't.

When he shook Sarah Johansen's hand, it was far too rough and calloused for so pretty a woman. Sarah had been working the fields, toiling behind a plow team when she should be no more concerned about anything than with what dress to wear on a given day.

To Cord there was no understanding why a man would want to break his back for years on end to grow something in the ground. Sarah Johansen worked the fields with her husband, and for what?

Calluses on your hands?

One new dress every two or three years?

The range war everyone knew was coming?

She seemed to blush when he shook her hand and the tinted color only added to her natural beauty.

The line jumped and Cord snapped from his thoughts, grabbed it and yanked his supper to the grass.

The fish were very nearly cooked in the fry pan over the campfire. Cord flipped them with the bayonet to allow them to cook a few more minutes and rolled a smoke to wait.

Night had fallen, the moon hadn't risen yet and the only light around Cord came from the fire. He felt the heat on his face.

When he shook Sarah's hand he felt a similar heat inside his stomach. She must have felt it also, or why did she blush so?

The fish started to crackle in the pan so he lifted it by the handle and set it on the ground to cool off a bit.

Cord never had much need or room in his life for a woman to call his own. He lived off the back of his horse, and his profession was too dangerous for him to take on a wife or even enter into a serious relationship.

Maybe when the herd was large enough and he retired to his property in California and built his ranch, his mind would change. Maybe then he could find a woman of his own to settle down with.

One as pretty as Sarah Johansen.

One who would blush at the touch of his hand.

Cord was suddenly annoyed with himself for allowing his thoughts to drift back over to a woman who wasn't his and was married with a boy to boot.

He grabbed the metal flask that contained bourbon whiskey and poured two ounces or so into the fry pan to soak the fish. He ate, sipping from the flask, and afterward rinsed the pan in the creek before settling into the lean-to.

How in the hell did shaking a woman's hand rattle him so, make him feel something he hadn't felt since he was a kid during the war.

Loneliness.


Sarah tossed and turned in the dark, willing her mind to sleep, but it just wouldn't obey her command. She told herself it was because James was away and the large bed felt so cold and empty.

She told herself.

The truth was that every time she closed her eyes, she saw his face and felt his touch on her hand.

It made her feel uneasy, like a stupid schoolgirl back in the

Great Woods of Wisconsin.

Married eleven years and with an eight-year-old son, a devoted husband, a farm and property, and she was thinking about another man's steel-gray eyes and the electricity she felt at his touch.

She wished she had gone to Minneapolis with James to the Grange.

She wished he was home right now and beside her, snoring lightly the way he did when he slept on his back. She would nudge him gently in the ribs with her elbow and he would roll over and quit snoring.

Sometimes James would roll back over and snore so loudly he would wake himself up and she would have to contain the laugh in her throat.

Enough acting like a child. Tomorrow was going to be a very long, hot and tiresome day. It would be even more so without a night's rest.

The fields needed checking, rocks needed to be picked up and hauled away, and if it didn't rain she and Seth would have to fill every receptacle they owned at the pump and haul them to the fields and water the crops by hand.

Sarah finally felt herself start to drift away, when Seth knocked on the door and announced that he didn't feel well.

# Twenty-Eight

Before sunup Cord broke camp and packed everything on his horse, figuring to make camp after visiting a few of the farmhouses on Teasel's list. The furthermost farm was six hours due west. If he followed the road for several hours and then turned north and west, he would reach the farm well before noon and have half the afternoon to backtrack to another farm.

Breakfast consisted of coffee and hard biscuits wrapped in brown paper he bought at the general store in town. There were six of them, and he ate four with his coffee, saving two to eat with some jerked beef later, when he was in the saddle.

He rode about six miles west on the road and spotted a cloud of dust racing toward him in one big hurry.

Cord broke his horse into a medium trot. After a few minutes the cloud of dust became a wagon traveling as fast as the two horses pulling it could go.

He slowed his horse to a stop on the road. When the wagon was close enough, he saw it was being driven by Sarah Johansen.

She spotted Cord and yanked hard on the reins to slow the team to a stop six or seven feet from him.

"Sarah, what are you doing?" Cord said.

"My son is very ill," Sarah said. "I'm taking him into town to see the barber."

Cord dismounted and walked to the wagon. Seth, wrapped in blankets full of ice chips, was asleep or unconscious. Cord felt the boy.

"Burning up," Cord said.

"I think it's his appendix," Sarah said.

Cord gently touched the left side of Seth's abdomen and the boy moaned softly in his sleep.

"Please move your horse so I can be on my way," Sarah said.

Cord looked at the team. "If you ride them another mile, both will be dead," he said. "Those are plow horses, not racers."

"Then I'll carry him," Sarah said.

"Not another six miles you won't," Cord said. "I'll take him."

"You?"

"Get down and give me a hand," Cord said.

Sarah stepped down from the buckboard. Cord removed a slice of rope from his saddlebags and gave it to her.

"I'll lift him to my saddle," Cord said. "Tie his hands to the horn."

Cord hoisted Seth from the wagon and gently placed him on the saddle. Sarah knotted Seth's hands to the horn with the rope.

Cord removed a thick brush from his saddlebags and gave it to Sarah.

"Brush the salt off your team and let them cool off at least thirty minutes before you move them again," Cord said. "Is this barber any good at doctoring?"

"He studied medicine in Baltimore," Sarah said.

"What's he doing barbering out here?"

"Ask him," Sarah said.

Cord mounted his horse behind Seth. "I'll get him there," he said. "Don't worry and don't kill your team rushing in, or you'll be pulling the wagon home yourself."

Sarah nodded. "Thank you."

Cord touched the brim of his hat and then kicked his horse into a full-blown run.

★ ★ ★ ★ ★

The barber's name was Coy, and he'd studied three years at a Baltimore medical school before dropping out due to an opium addiction he developed during the beginning of his fourth year of study. He came west ten years ago to beat his addiction and get a clean start.

He got both.

Coy was in the middle of shaving Sheriff Smiley when Cord kicked open the door to his shop with the Johansen boy in his arms.

"Got a sick boy here," Cord said.

Coy pointed to a curtain that led to the back room.

"Put him on the table," Coy said.

"It's his appendix, all right," Coy said. "And it has to come out right now or it will burst and this boy will die."

"Can you do it?" Cord said.

Coy nodded. "Where's the boy's mother?"

"I met her on the road," Cord said. "She was killing her team getting here. She won't be here for at least two hours or so."

"Can't wait," Coy said. "Go wash your hands with soap in the basin and then pour whiskey over them from the bottle there on the table. You're going to assist me."

Cord was eating a steak and coffee in the hotel dining room when Sarah walked in and stood over the table.

The dining room was full, and an immediate buzz ran through the room.

"Mr. Coy said my son will be fine," Sarah said. "I wanted to thank you for what you did. Mr. Coy said another hour and Seth might have died."

"Sit and have a cup of coffee with me," Cord said.

Sarah looked across the room at the waitress and nodded.

Then she took a seat. The buzz in the room turned to hushed whispering.

The waitress arrived at the table.

"Coffee for Mrs. Johansen," Cord said.

The waitress nodded and went to get a second cup. She returned in a moment with the cup and filled it from a pot.

"Mrs. Johansen," the waitress said, nodded and walked away.

"I'm afraid the gossip squad is out in full bloom," Sarah said as she lifted her cup.

Cord looked around the room at the gossipers. Eyes immediately averted from him and looked away.

Cord stood up from the table. "Attention, everybody in the room," he said in a thunderous voice. "I met Mrs. Johansen on the road into town. Her boy was very sick with appendicitis. He wouldn't have survived the trip into town in the back of the wagon. I took the boy to see Mr. Coy on my horse, and he removed the boy's appendix. Mrs. Johansen stopped by to thank me, so you can all put your gossiping tongues back in your mouths."

Cord sat and picked up his coffee cup and took a sip.

Sarah stifled a laugh as she looked around the room.

Cord winked at her, and she felt a blush on her neck that she hoped he didn't notice—at the same time she wanted him to.

At that moment, Coy entered the dining room and approached the table.

"Seth will be awake inside of thirty minutes," Coy said. "You can go sit with him if you like."

Sarah nodded and stood up. "Thank you again, Mr. Cord," she said and extended her right hand.

Cord took it and shook gently. "You're welcome."

After Sarah left the room, Coy sat and waved the waitress to the table. "Coffee, please," he said.

She brought a cup to the table and filled it.

Coy took a sip and looked at Cord. "I didn't recognize you right off," he said. "You're the gun hand Parker hired, aren't you? I saw you that day on the street when you broke up the whipping. The Parker boy got less than he deserved if you ask me."

"I took a job for Parker," Cord said. "I couldn't say about the gun hand part."

"Well, gun hand or not, that Johansen boy owes you his life," Coy said.

"You did that," Cord said. "All I did was hand you instruments and wipe up blood."

"You got him to me in time," Coy said. "You didn't have to do that."

"Yeah, I did," Cord said.

Seth opened his eyes and was disoriented and out of focus.

Sarah said, "Seth, can you hear me?"

Slowly Seth's eyes focused on Sarah.

"Ma, what happened?" Seth said.

"You got sick with what they call appendicitis," Sarah said. "You could have died, but Mr. Coy removed your appendix, and you'll be all right."

"You mean took it out of me?" Seth said.

Sarah smiled brightly. "That's exactly what I mean," she said.

# TWENTY-NINE

Having lost so much of the day, Cord was able to make just one farm before sunset. Family named Dufraine, consisting of husband, wife and four children. They had two hundred acres of prime land and were averaging five hundred dollars a year in income. They had no use for Parker and his deals.

Cord expected no less from the Dufraine family. Mr. Dufraine said he would attend the meeting when Johansen returned from the Grange, but also said not to expect him to change his mind anytime soon.

"I fought in the war," Dufraine said. "I ain't afraid of a little gunplay. You tell Parker that for me."

Cord made camp for the night near a shallow creek. He built a fire, tended to his horse and then assembled the lean-to and prepared a supper of bacon, baked beans, biscuits and coffee.

Afterward, he rolled a cigarette, leaned against his saddle and smoked the cigarette as he looked up at the stars. The sky was clear, and there were literally too many to count, so he concentrated on the stars he recognized.

The Great Bear.

Leo.

Orion.

Gemini.

The planet Venus.

The North Star.

On a clear night like this one, Cord could navigate by the stars and not get lost. He could even tell the time to within fifteen minutes or so of the hour by their placement in the sky.

He looked for shooting stars, and every few minutes would spot one silently streaking across the sky only to vanish a moment later.

He was filling his mind with thoughts to occupy it besides Sarah Johansen.

The shy way she looked around the dining room when she spoke of the gossiping going on at the other tables.

She wasn't his and never would be, so Cord told himself to quit wasting time thinking about her, and he went to sleep.

Sarah made arrangements to stay at Mrs. Cullen's boarding house at the end of Main Street where the three-story home sat by itself. Mr. Coy told her that Seth couldn't be moved for three days, so she asked Mrs. Cullen to put her up for the night. She let her have a top-floor room for seventy-five cents, plus fifty cents extra for breakfast.

The room was stifling hot, but it had a balcony with a rocking chair, so she sat out a while to enjoy the cooler night air. Soft piano music sounded from the saloon at the opposite end of Main Street.

What happened today gave her pause. Seth could have died because they lived so far from town—and a town without a real doctor, to boot. It was dumb luck or God's will that Mr. Cord happened to be traveling on the same road at the same time as she.

He was right when he said she would have killed the horses running them the way that she had. After he left with Seth, she brushed them down with his brush. They were lathered in thick, salty sweat. Another mile at the pace she was pushing the massive plow horses, and they would have collapsed from heatstroke.

Where would she have been then, miles from town without horses and Seth as sick as he was?

Maybe when James returned, they should give Parker's offer some considerable thought. Not that she thought Parker was right and they wrong, but they could use the money to relocate somewhere not so remote and where a doctor made house calls.

She remembered that she didn't return Mr. Cord's brush. It was still in the wagon. She must remember to give it to him when he attended the meeting when James returned from the Grange.

Sarah looked up at the night sky, at the millions of visible stars. She took little comfort in their beauty.

Her chest ached, and she didn't know why.

That was a lie.

She knew exactly why her chest ached, and she felt ashamed at her own thoughts.

The best thing to do was get some sleep and spend tomorrow morning with Seth before returning to the farm.

Sarah went to bed where, after much tossing and turning, she finally drifted off to a restless sleep.

# THIRTY

After three hard days and nights in the saddle, Cord rode back to Brooks to meet with Parker.

Fourteen of fourteen farmers had rejected the offer to sell their land.

That wouldn't sit well with Parker.

Less so for his son.

The gunplay, it seemed, was destined to happen.

Men like Parker didn't understand the meaning of the word no, and his son was just careless and stupid enough to ignite things on his own. People on both sides would die, and for what?

Greed for land?

Foolish, stubborn pride?

Maybe both?

As he rode, Cord thought about a solution to the problem that would minimize bloodshed. The thing of it was, once that first shot was fired and blood spilled, it started a chain reaction that was almost impossible to stop. Like that first shot fired in war. A thousand soon followed.

James stepped off the stagecoach and spotted Sarah in the wagon across the street. He felt like running to her and giving her a big squeeze. Sarah frowned upon such public displays of affection, so he resisted the urge and calmly carried his bag to the wagon, set it in back and climbed aboard next to her.

131

They kissed lightly.

"Seth doing his chores?" James said.

"Before I answer that, how did it go with the Grange?" Sarah said.

"Couldn't have gone better," James said.

Sarah handed the reins to James.

"I'll tell you about it on the way home," she said.

"How do you feel, son?" James said as he stood over Seth's bed.

"Hungry, Pa," Seth said.

"Your ma is fixing us all some lunch," James said.

"Can I get out of bed?"

"I'll ask your ma," James said.

Seth was able to walk on his own steam to the table and ate a hearty lunch with James and Sarah. Afterward, feeling a bit tired, Seth returned to bed for a nap.

James and Sarah took coffee to the porch.

James filled his pipe and lit it with a wood match.

"I'm having a hard time understanding why Parker's hired gun would put himself out to save our boy the way he did," James said. "That just doesn't make sense to me."

"It was just coincidence that we met on the road, James," Sarah said. "And as I told you riding home, he didn't strike me so much as a hired killer, but more like a businessman hired by Parker to settle a dispute."

"I understand that, but what concerns me is how he will settle the dispute," James said. "A gunfighter knows only one way to end an argument."

"When will you have the meeting about the Grange?" Sarah said. "If what you told me is true, the Grange can put a stop to Parker's threats."

"I'll start spreading the word tomorrow morning," James

said. "Mal's place is more central. If he's willing, we'll hold the meeting there."

Sarah nodded and then stood up. "I best check on Seth," she said and went inside.

James smoked his pipe and tried to make sense of the recent events. First a stranger stops Mal Jones from a whipping, the same stranger turns out to be Parker's hired gunfighter, and then he turns right around and saves his boy.

Why?

Even if it was a coincidental meeting on the road, why would a hired gunfighter care enough what happened to a small boy to do what he did?

James didn't realize his pipe had gone out until he tried to draw in smoke and sucked nothing but air. He opened his tin matchbox, withdrew a wood match and relit the pipe.

There was time to check the fields before the cow needed milking. He stood and walked down the steps to the wagon, hitched the team and called out to Sarah.

She came to the door.

"Be back in time to milk the cow," James said. "I want to check the fields."

Sarah nodded and closed the door.

James was walking the pumpkin field when he heard a horse to his left and did a quick turnabout.

A man dressed in black trail clothes with long hair and a dark beard sat in the saddle watching him.

"Are you James Johansen?" he said.

James looked at the man's sidearm and knew by sight he was Cord, Parker's gunfighter.

"I'm not toting iron," James said.

Cord lifted one leg over the saddle and seemed to slide to the ground with the grace of a cat. He removed the gun belt and

133

shoulder holster and hung both on the saddle horn.

"Okay to come down and talk?" Cord said.

"Come ahead, but be careful of my crops," James said.

Cord walked down the hill, followed the dirt path that separated the fields and finally stopped a few feet from James.

"I'm Cord. I work for Mr. Parker," Cord said.

"I know," James said. "I'm grateful to you for saving my son's life. That doesn't change anything between me and Parker. I feel you should know that."

"One has nothing to do with the other," Cord said. "I've been visiting all the farms, telling the farmers about Parker's offer. I figure you and the others will hold a meeting about the Grange. I told them I would attend and take back to Parker your decision."

James studied Cord for a moment. The man was a good six or seven inches taller than he, and broad at the shoulder, with lean, hard muscle making up most of him. He reminded James of a sleeping rattlesnake that dared you to awaken him.

"If our decision doesn't please Parker?" James said.

"One way or another, he aims to have this land," Cord said.

"I know what one way is. What's the other?" James said.

"It occurs to me, looking at your fields, that if you put some rain barrels on the end of each field, drilled some holes in them and sealed them with corks, you could water your crops during a drought," Cord said. "All you'd need is a ramp under each barrel."

"You know irrigation?" James said.

"Some."

"I got enough barrels in the barn," James said. "What I don't got is another man to help, and it's a two-man job."

"When do you think you might have that meeting?" Cord said.

"Day after next," James said.

"Where?"

"Mal Jones's farm, probably."

"I'll see you there."

"Now wait a second. Please," James said. "You said one thing's got nothing to do with the other, and I agree to that point. Why don't you come home with me and have supper with us. My son would like to thank you proper for saving his life, and my wife is a mighty fair cook."

"So long as you remember we're on the opposite end of things," Cord said.

"If I forget, you can remind me," James said.

Sarah was peeling potatoes on the porch when she heard the wagon arrive and nearly cut a finger with the knife when she saw Cord seated next to James on the buckboard.

Behind the wagon, Cord's horse was tethered. He stopped when the wagon stopped.

James hopped down and said, "I'll unhitch the team. You can put your horse in the corral and wash up at the pump."

Cord stepped down, freed his horse and walked it to the corral while James unhitched the team.

"James?" Sarah said.

"Be right there, hon," James said.

"Now, James," Sarah said.

James left the team and went up to the porch.

"What is that man doing here?" Sarah said.

"I invited him to supper."

"A hired killer? To eat at our table?"

"He ain't even wearing his guns," James said. "And Seth wanted to thank him. Well, now is his chance."

"I'll set an extra plate, then," Sarah said, coldly.

James kissed her lightly on the lips and then went to tend to the team.

While James walked the team into the barn, Cord locked his horse in the corral and slung his saddle over the fence. Then he walked to the pump and pulled his shirt overhead and set it aside on the bucket beside the pump.

Cord's stomach was a flat wall of hard rigid muscle. His arms, chest and shoulders tightened and bulged as he cranked the pump and tossed cold water on his face and some on his chest and under his arms.

Trying to peel potatoes and watch Cord at the same time, Sarah nicked her finger and a droplet of blood appeared.

She sucked the blood and looked at Cord as he didn't bother to dry off but pulled his shirt back over his head. He looked at her and walked to the porch but didn't take the steps up.

"I don't have a clean shirt to wear at your table," he said. "I apologize for that."

Sarah looked at Cord. He smiled at her, and she quickly looked away to avoid blushing. "No need," she said.

James came up behind Cord. "No need of what?" James said.

"I don't have a clean shirt to wear to supper," Cord said.

"I think we can look the other way this one time," James said.

Sarah glared at James. "I have to see to Seth, and then I'll start on supper," she said. "You men can sit and have coffee while you wait."

When Sarah called the men into supper, James was pleased to see she used the fine dinnerware they received from her parents as wedding gifts. Dinner was fried chicken, mashed potatoes with gravy, carrots and apple pie for dessert. Sarah gave the men the choice of water with ice, milk or coffee with the meal. Cord chose milk, which somehow surprised her.

Seth stared at Cord as they ate supper. Seth didn't know what to expect from Cord, but the gunfighter ate slowly and almost delicately, like his ma.

When she did allow herself to glance at Cord, Sarah noticed his fine table manners as well, and wished that James was a bit more delicate at mealtime.

Seth's curiosity got the better of him and he blurted out, "Where are your guns?"

"Seth!" Sarah scolded him.

"That's all right, Mrs. Johansen," Cord said. "I left them outside with my saddle. Unless supper was served still alive and kicking and you wanted me to shoot it, I figured I wouldn't need them."

Seth stared at Cord. "Still alive?" he said.

James shook his head as he laughed.

Sarah tried her best to glare at Cord, but her lips quivered and she joined James in laughing.

After supper was finished, Sarah cleared the table and served the apple pie with coffee and milk for Seth. The pie was still warm and its aroma filled the house.

"Can I have a big piece, Ma?" Seth said.

"I think one bellyache this week is enough," Sarah said.

Sarah sliced the pie and served it on the plates her mother gave them as wedding gifts. For the coffee, she used the matching cups and saucers.

"This is really good pie, Mrs. Johansen, and it was a really elegant dinner," Cord said when he tasted the pie.

Sarah felt her neck flush and she hid it by placing her right hand to her neck.

Thank God, James didn't notice.

"When will you see Parker?" James said.

"James, no talk of that in the house," Sarah said. "Seth, help me clean the table."

Cord stood up and looked at Sarah. "Thank you again, Mrs. Johansen," he said. He looked at James. "I'll see Parker in the morning and tell him how things are."

"Stay the night in the barn," James said. "It's dark soon."

Sarah felt a twinge in her stomach at that.

"I don't mind night riding at all," Cord said. "Good night."

As Cord walked to the door, Seth turned to James. "Can I see him to his horse, Pa? Please."

James nodded. "Then come right back and get into bed. You don't want to bust open those stitches."

Seth walked slightly behind Cord until they reached the corral. As Cord opened the gate to get his horse, Seth stood on a rail to watch Cord saddle the brown stallion. Once he had the saddle in place, Cord walked the horse out and closed the gate.

"It's dark," Seth said.

"I don't mind the dark," Cord said.

Seth watched as Cord removed the shoulder holster from the saddle horn and attached it to his left shoulder. Once the rig was in place, he gave it a tug to tighten the fit.

"What if your horse steps in a hole and trips?" Seth said.

Cord grabbed his holster from the saddle horn. "He won't."

A strange thing happened then as Cord slipped the holster around his waist in a smooth, practiced motion. To Seth, putting the massive sidearm on seemed to transform Cord from friendly dinner guest to dangerous gunman. The most dangerous man Seth had ever seen up close.

"Good night, son," Cord said as he mounted his horse with the grace of a cat.

"Thank you again for saving me," Seth said.

"You can return the favor," Cord said.

"How?"

"When you grow up to be a man, you can take care of your folks," Cord said, and then with a slight movement of his body, the horse turned and they rode away into the darkness.

★ ★ ★ ★ ★

Sarah walked into the dark bedroom and softly closed the door. Bright moonlight came through the open window, and she could see James asleep in the bed. She stood over James and gently shook him awake.

James opened his eyes. "Something wrong with Seth?"

"No."

Sarah pulled the long nightshirt over her head and tossed it over a chair. She wore nothing underneath.

"What are you . . . ?" James said.

"We need a son," Sarah said.

"Right now?" James said.

"Yes," Sarah said as she flung the covers off James. "Right now."

# THIRTY-ONE

Cord met with Parker in the rancher's office in town. Parker's son John and Teasel were present as well.

Cord sat in a chair opposite Parker's desk. John Parker and Teasel stood off to the side behind Cord.

"I expect I already know the outcome of the meeting the farmers will hold come Wednesday," Parker said after Cord gave him his report.

"I expect so," Cord said.

"I am not without my own resources, Mr. Cord," Parker said. "You tell these farmers that a representative of the Cattlemen's Association and the lieutenant governor of Wyoming Territory will be coming to Brooks on Friday to meet with me personally. Tell them to be very careful of the decision they arrive at because they will have to live with the consequences."

"I'll tell them that," Cord said.

"I expect you to report to me directly after that meeting," Parker said.

Cord nodded and stood up.

"Pa, we don't need this Yankee scum to settle our fights," John said.

Cord turned and looked at John.

"Shut up, John," Parker said.

"What did you call me?" Cord said.

Standing beside John, Teasel moved out of the way.

"You heard me," John said. "I ain't forgot how you cheap-shot me on the street that day. You're not just Yankee scum, you're a coward. My father don't see it, but I sure can. It's all over town how you brought in the Johansen boy on . . ."

Cord moved so quickly, Teasel and Parker didn't have time to blink.

Cord smacked John across the face with so much force that John bent over like a thin reed in the wind. Before John could straighten up, Cord snatched the gun in John's holster and tossed it on Parker's desk, then grabbed John's shirt and flung him into the wall and pressed his weight against John's back.

"Mr. Parker, am I excused?" Cord said.

"You are," Parker said.

Cord released John, turned and walked out of the office.

John came off the wall and went to reach for his gun.

"Pick that up and he will kill you for sure, John," Parker said.

Teasel put a hand on John's shoulder. "Best sit down and cool off," Teasel said.

Parker looked at Teasel. "Take my son over to the saloon and buy him a cold beer," he said. "When he's cooled off enough, give him his gun back."

"What did you mean by Yankee scum?" Teasel said.

"When I was out getting signatures for Pa's petition, I sent out some telegrams myself checking on Mr. Gunfighter," John said. "He fought with the Union army against the South. Rode with Sherman into Georgia in sixty-four."

"So did a half million other men. So what?" Teasel said.

"He's from Missouri," John said. "He turned on his own kind to fight with the Union. You can never trust a man who turns against his own kind."

"Now you listen to me, John," Teasel said. "You don't know nothing about that man, and you best keep it that way if you want to grow to be a nice old and very rich rancher the way your pa intends you to be. You get under Cord's burr one more time, and it won't be his backhand he draws."

"Pa intends nothing for me," John said. "He hates me, and don't think I don't know it."

"If you think that, you're a bigger fool than I thought," Teasel said. "Finish your beer. We got work to do."

# THIRTY-TWO

James barely had his eyes open when Sarah rolled over on top of him.

"Woman, we just did . . . ," James said.

Sarah held him tight and pressed her body against his.

"James, I can't explain it to you, but I need to have a second son," Sarah whispered.

"I have to get to the meeting at Mal's place," James said.

"Five minutes is all we need," Sarah said.

"Well, let me get my shirt off," James said.

By noon, fourteen farmers and their families had gathered in the front yard of Mal Jones's farm. A long table was set up with pots of coffee, fresh toasted bread, several pies, lemonade, coffee and tea.

James chaired the meeting. His first order of business was to formally introduce Cord as an official representative of Jefferson Parker.

Cord stood beside James, and his height was obvious to all as he stood next to the much shorter farmer.

"I been to your farms and met all of you over the past week," Cord said. "I met with Mr. Parker only yesterday, and I will bring him your decision on selling him your land. I won't try to influence how you vote on his proposal, but let me speak plain. Mr. Parker is not a man that takes kindly to rejection when he wants something. He has the political power of the Cattlemen's

Association and the territorial governor on his side, and they all want the same thing. That is statehood for Wyoming. If you vote to stay, then I suggest that if you aren't prepared for a fight, you get your mind around the fact that one is coming."

"Is that a threat?" a farmer named Hogan said.

"No," Cord said. "I'm not here to threaten you. I'm just telling you how things are. If you know Parker at all, then you know I'm telling you the truth."

"You're saying Parker will drive us out with gunplay?" a farmer named Boyle said.

"I'm not saying one way or the other what Parker will do. That's up to him," Cord said. "What I am saying is to be prepared to deal with the consequences of how you vote on his offer."

"I say the hell with him and his offer," a farmer named Sanders shouted and then spat on the ground.

"No call for that," James said.

"I said my piece, so I'll just sit quietly in the background while you have your meeting. Then I'll take Parker your decision," Cord said.

Cord took a chair from the table and moved it back away from the crowd and sat. He pulled out his tobacco pouch to roll a cigarette and noticed Sarah watching him. He nodded to her.

She quickly turned her eyes away and looked at James.

"To be fair to all, I think everyone with a stake in this should speak his piece before we put things to a vote," James said.

"Maybe you should speak about the Grange first?" Uggla suggested.

"All right," James said.

Keri Jones went around the table with a fresh pot of coffee to fill cups. Sarah noticed another full pot on the other end of the table and assisted Keri in filling cups. Sarah filled a half dozen cups and then lifted an unused cup, filled it and carried it to Cord.

Cord took the cup and locked eyes with Sarah. Her cheeks reddened and she quickly turned away and went back to the table.

James spoke for twenty minutes on his meeting with the Grange. Their application for membership was granted. That gave them political power, if not equal to the Cattlemen's Association, then at least enough to thwart a direct threat. As more and more farmers in Wyoming applied for membership, the Grange would grow in numbers and at some point be equal to the Cattlemen's Association. When that happened, both rancher and farmer would be forced to coexist out of necessity.

Statehood wasn't but a decade or less away, and neither the Grange nor the Cattlemen's Association wanted a war between the two organizations in which Washington would be forced to intercede and settle. That would set statehood back years.

"I won't speak for any family here, but I bought and paid for my land and have worked it sunup to sundown to make it work. Nobody is going to force me to leave the home I built for me and my family," James said. "I'll go out in a pine box before I see that happen."

"I believe we all feel the same way," Mal Jones said.

"Let's quit wasting time and put it to a vote," Uggla said.

Every man voted no and signed their names to a paper rejecting Parker's offer to buy their land at any price.

James gave Cord the document.

"Take this to Parker and tell him our decision," James said. "You can also tell him we have the Grange on our side, and things won't sit well with them in Washington if he persists in trying to squeeze us out."

Cord stood and looked at the group.

"I will tell him," Cord said. "But let me ask you this. Will you be willing to meet with Parker to talk things over and see if some kind of agreement can be reached that is helpful to both sides?"

James looked at his friends and neighbors. "Where would this meeting take place?"

"In his office in town this Friday," Cord said. "The lieutenant territorial governor and a representative from the Cattlemen's Association will be there as well. It's an opportunity to air your differences to the opposition in a somewhat legal setting."

"James is our delegate to the Grange," Uggla said. "I think he speaks for us all."

James nodded. "I'll attend the meeting," he said. "And then we'll meet again at Mal's place to discuss the results. Fair?"

Cord nodded.

The group watched as Cord walked to his horse, mounted up and rode off along the road.

"What kind of agreement do you think Parker will be willing to reach?" Uggla said.

"Most likely that gunfighter will be told to turn his guns against us," Boyle said. "Then what? I haven't fired a gun in ten years at anything other than a turkey."

"None of us are gunmen here," James said. "But we have the law on our side and a voice in Washington and Casper to listen to us. They can't shoot the law off the books."

"Maybe they can't shoot the law," Boyle said. "But they can shoot us."

# Thirty-Three

The sun was barely up when Seth finished feeding the chickens. He was about to enter the barn to milk the cow when he spotted something down the road that he couldn't make out because it was still too dark to see properly.

He walked to the edge of the road and squinted at the moving object. All of a sudden he recognized Mr. Cord on his horse.

Seth turned and sprinted all the way into the house.

Pa was washing his face at the kitchen pump. Ma was pouring coffee, as breakfast was close to being on the table.

"Ma, Pa!" Seth shouted as he barged into the house.

"Unless something broke its leg, there is no need to shout," James said.

"It's Mr. Cord. He's riding in," Seth said.

James wiped his hands on a towel. "Well, let's see what he wants."

James and Seth went outside. Sarah set the coffeepot on the table, turned and walked into the bedroom. She stood before the half-length mirror on the back of the door. Her hair was a bit of a mess so she straightened it a bit. Her apron was covered with flour and she removed it.

Her heart was beating like a rabbit in her chest, and her cheeks and neck were suddenly flushed.

"Oh, you stupid woman," Sarah said aloud and returned to the kitchen.

★ ★ ★ ★ ★

James and Seth waited on the porch for Cord to arrive.

He rode up in no hurry, dismounted at the corral and tied the reins to the fence rail.

"Morning," Cord said as he walked to the porch.

"Morning," James said. "And I have to say it's a bit of a surprise seeing you again so soon."

"I met with Parker," Cord said. "I figured we could talk before you see him tomorrow."

"Stay for breakfast," James said. "We'll discuss things afterward."

Seth, transfixed on Cord's guns, watched as Cord removed them and hung them over the porch railing.

Sarah was standing behind the table with her arms behind her back when James and Seth escorted Cord into the house.

A fourth plate was set next to Seth's.

"Good morning, Mrs. Johansen," Cord said.

"Good morning," Sarah said. "I took the liberty of setting a place for you for breakfast."

"Thank you," Cord said.

"Well, let's sit before it gets cold," James said.

Sarah served the eggs, bacon, potatoes, toasted bread, coffee and milk for Seth.

Seth had a hundred questions for Cord, but he held his tongue as Cord and James engaged in conversation.

"I can't pay a man outright to help harvest the second field, but I can offer him half the profits when we bring that field to market," James said.

"Sharecropping," Cord said.

"I get the feeling you know more about farming than you let on," James said.

"I've done some in my youth," Cord said.

"You was a farmer?" Seth said.

"Were, Seth," Sarah said. "Remember your English."

Cord smiled at Seth and winked at the boy.

Seth smiled at Cord.

Sarah looked down at the table.

When breakfast was finished, James said, "Let's take our coffee to the porch. I can smoke my pipe and you can tell me what Parker said."

Seth jumped to his feet.

James looked at Seth. "You stay and help your ma with the dishes."

"Let him go, James," Sarah said. "He's heard everything said at the meeting and is growing up quickly."

James nodded. "But no coffee," he said. "He ain't growing up that quickly."

"Parker plans to offer five thousand dollars to any farmer willing to sell," Cord said. "He will make that offer on Friday at the meeting. He asked me to give you advance notice so you can sleep on it."

"He needs the land that badly?" James said.

"Parker plans to double the size of his herd. In order to do that, he needs every available acre and drop of water running through it," Cord said. "For Parker it's not just about getting you and the others to move out, but about keeping others from moving in."

James sucked on his pipe and blew smoke.

"This is a big country," James said. "There ought to be room for all of us to exist together, if it weren't for the greed in some men's hearts."

Cord, smoking a rolled cigarette, blew smoke and said, "Well, there it is. I hope things can be worked out tomorrow."

James nodded. "Well, my farm ain't going to tend to itself."

"Isn't," Seth said.

James faked an angry stare at Seth. "Your ma's been teaching you English again, huh, son?"

"I have nothing to do and nobody to do it with until tomorrow," Cord said. "How about I work off that fine breakfast your wife made and we take those rain barrels out to your field?"

James looked at Cord. "You want to help me with farm work?"

"Dirty fingernails never hurt anybody," Cord said.

"Can I help too, Pa?" Seth said.

"I'll be damned," James said. "Go tell your ma we'll be needing lunch for three."

James and Cord carried four barrels from the barn to the outside water pump. James didn't have a hose, so they had to fill each barrel halfway at the pump and lift them onto the wagon.

Even half full, each barrel weighed three hundred pounds. It was no easy chore to load the four of them onto the wagon.

"To save weight, I'll ride Seth out on my horse," Cord said. "We'll ride behind to keep an eye on the wagon."

Sarah watched from the kitchen window as James and Cord filled and loaded barrels onto the wagon. She kept hidden by the yellow curtains covering the window, feeling silly and foolish, like a school girl with a crush on a boy.

When the men and Seth finished loading and rode off, Sarah sat at the table and was finally able to shake the butterflies out of her stomach. Then she stood and stacked the clean dishes on the shelf above the sink and went to the bedroom.

She looked in the mirror again and decided to brush her hair. She was a fright to look at with her apron and messy hair and . . .

"Remember that you are a married woman," she said aloud.

"And a foolish one at that."

After placing one barrel at each end of two fields, James, Cord and Seth set about digging an irrigation ditch the length of each field. It was hot, and after a short time they removed their shirts.

By noon they had accomplished quite a bit and decided to take a break and wait for Sarah to arrive with lunch.

Ten minutes or so later, Seth cried, "Pa, is that Ma coming?"

Sarah, wearing her dungaree pants and work shirt and boots and carrying a picnic basket in one hand and an extra hoe in the other, strolled toward them along the road. She had her hair up and covered by a yellow straw sun hat.

"What do you think you are doing?" James said when Sarah arrived.

"Bringing lunch," Sarah said.

"Sometimes you beat all," James said.

"I rode Mr. Cord's horse," Seth told Sarah.

"Maybe you can thank him by giving him a sandwich," Sarah said.

After lunch, they worked another five hours digging trenches alongside the rows of growing crops. Sarah worked a middle row and whenever she could, she stole a glance at Cord.

Cord worked tirelessly, and although his upper body was drenched in sweat, he never seemed to grow fatigued. Occasionally he would look up to check his work, and once or twice he caught her stealing a glance.

Red in the face, Sarah quickly returned to her digging.

Around five in the afternoon, the work was done and James explained to Sarah how the barrels would work.

"Once I buy some spigots at Tobey's I'll drill a hole in each barrel low enough for gravity to feed the water," James said. "I'll build a ramp from the spigots to the ditch and open each one, water will flow down the ramp and into the ditches and water the crops. One or two good rainfalls, and each barrel should be full."

"So if we have a drought, the crops won't die," Seth said.

"That's right, son," James said.

"And we won't starve," Seth said.

"Also right."

Cord slipped his shirt on and grabbed his guns off the back of his horse. "I best get moving," he said as he slid the gun belt around his waist and second belt over the left shoulder.

"What about supper? Can you stay for supper?" Seth said.

"Afraid not," Cord said. He looked Sarah in the eyes. "Thank you for breakfast and the picnic lunch."

"We should thank you for the work you've done," Sarah said.

"Seth, get in the wagon," James said.

Cord mounted his horse and looked at James. "See you in the morning," he said and broke the horse into a full trot.

James helped Sarah into the wagon and then climbed up beside her. Seth rode in back with the tools.

"I think I might shave and take a bath tonight so I look presentable at that meeting," James said.

Sarah touched James on the arm.

"That would be nice," she said.

# THIRTY-FOUR

James wore clean pants, a freshly laundered blue shirt and boots polished by Sarah the night before.

Parker stood from behind his oak desk and nodded to James when he entered Parker's office.

"For the record, in attendance at this meeting are Lieutenant Governor Paul Grover, Cattlemen's Association Representative from Washington Edward White, Sheriff Smiley, sheriff of Brooks, my son John, ranch foreman Teasel, myself and James Johansen, acting as the representative for the Grange," Parker said.

James looked at the woman seated at a small table beside the desk. She was scribbling in a notebook almost as quickly as Parker could speak.

"The lieutenant governor's private secretary," Parker said.

"Where's your man Cord?" James said.

"I felt it best, since he is not employed by Mr. Parker in any official capacity, that he not attend this meeting," Grover said.

"I see," James said.

"Shall we get started?" Parker said.

A long conference table with chairs was set up, centered in the large office. Pots of coffee with cups and silver creamers were on each end of the table.

Parker sat at the head of the table with Grover and White on each side of him. Grover's secretary stood up and served the coffee and then returned to her table and picked up her pencil.

153

"The matter before us this morning concerns my offer to purchase the farms surrounding my ranch plus the open ranges scattered between the farms," Parker said. "And its rejection by the owners of the farms, even though my offer of three thousand dollars per property represents ten years' income on average for each family."

Parker paused to allow the secretary to catch up, and when she was, she nodded.

"Now I'm not an unreasonable man, and I do understand the attachment a man can feel about something he built with his own two hands. However, it is my opinion that these farms, coupled with more farmers who surely will follow, will prevent Wyoming from achieving the statehood it deserves."

Parker glanced at the secretary. She was right with him.

"How do you figure that?" James said. "About preventing statehood I mean."

"This is cattle country, Mr. Johansen," White said. "It will ride those cattle to statehood and become an important beef-producing state in the Union. Farms, as valuable as they may be, are in the way here. It would be best for all concerned if you took Mr. Parker's generous offer and moved your farm to an agricultural state such as Ohio or Idaho."

"Best for you is what you mean," James said.

"Mr. Johansen, we have things tied up in Casper so that it would take years for any more land to be sold to farmers," White said. "The freight lines on which you ship your product for milling belong to Mr. Parker. This fall you will have to take your harvest to Medicine Bow to the railroad yourself in your own wagons, all of you. You might find that the general store will no longer sell to you on credit while you wait for the next harvest. One bad year and you, your family, and every other farmer in the area could starve. I doubt then that you would get so generous an offer from Mr. Parker."

"Three thousand per farm, and I will add five hundred dollars extra for moving expenses," Parker said.

"Take it, Mr. Johansen," White said. "The Grange isn't going to be of much help in this situation. At best, they could delay things a year or two in Washington with red tape, and by then you and your family will have been starved out and Mr. Parker will buy your land at auction when you can't pay the taxes."

James lifted the cup and took a sip. "This is delicious," he said. "What kind of coffee is this?"

Parker, White and Grover exchanged glances.

"This stupid farmer didn't hear one word you said," John said.

"That's enough out of you, boy," Parker said.

"I heard you," James said. "Every lying word. I bought my land, I work my land, my son will reach manhood on my land, and someday I'll be buried on my land. If we have to form a wagon train to take our harvest to market, then so be it. If there is such a drought that our crops wither and die, then so will your cattle, right along with our crops. And I'll tell you something else. If the Grange was as powerless in this situation as you say, Mr. White wouldn't be reduced to making hollow threats. I believe that I speak for the other thirteen families. Is there anything else?"

"I will go four thousand dollars plus moving expenses for each farmer," Parker said. "That's more money than you can make in a decade breaking your back to raise crops."

"Maybe so, but the crops I raise are mine," James said. "Not yours."

"I'm a reasonable man," Parker said. "Why can't you be reasonable as well?"

"Reasonable man?" James said. "A reasonable man would be satisfied with the great wealth that he already has and not look to take away what little others have for the sake of his own power. No, I think we're done here today."

"Mr. Johansen, don't you want Wyoming to become a state?" Grover said.

"I do, but not badly enough to sell out what I believe in," James said. "My conscience and my soul are worth more to me than statehood."

"And what about the others?" Grover said.

"They feel as I do," James said.

"Are you sure?" Grover said. "Maybe some of them wouldn't mind four thousand dollars and moving expenses."

"Five thousand," Parker said.

"There you go, five thousand and expenses," Grover said. "As the Grange representative, don't you owe it to the others to let them decide for themselves if they want to take it or leave it?"

James nodded. "I will tell the others of your offer. If some of them want to take it, that's up to them," he said. "Those who want to stay, that's also up to them, and I expect that decision to be honored as well. I can tell you right now that I'm staying, and the only way that I will leave is in a pine box."

"How soon can you speak to the others and get word to us?" White said.

"Monday morning soon enough?" James said.

"We'll stay over at the hotel," White said.

James stood and walked to the door.

"Mr. Johansen?" Parker said.

James turned back around.

"I will win this," Parker said. "One way or another."

"I can't say as I'm surprised," Parker said. He, Grover, White, John and Teasel had moved the meeting to the saloon where they drank cold beer.

"Pa, why don't we just drive them out and be done with it?" John said.

"I understand how you feel, son," White said. "I'm a cattleman at heart, but a range war and bloodshed won't sit well with Congress when they return in the fall. News like that would put statehood back ten years or more if they believe we're still a lawless territory not ready to join the Union."

"So we're going to let some sodbusters rule over us?" John said.

Grover looked at John and said, "This isn't about who can drive who out of the territory. Of course we can force them out, but that isn't how statehood is won anymore. This isn't eighteen forty-five, and we're not Texas. They say by nineteen hundred most states will have the telephone and electric lights instead of oil lamps. If we want to win this, we have to do it with the rule of law and not with the gun. Times are changing, and we need to change with them if we're to win statehood and survive as cattlemen."

John grabbed his beer and downed it in several long gulps, set the glass down, stood and said, "I have work to do on the ranch."

As John walked out of the saloon, Parker nodded to Teasel, and the ranch foreman got up to follow John.

"What about this man you hired?" White said.

"Cord? Do you know him?" Parker said.

"Only by reputation," White said. "I'm told he's as deadly as any man who walks the ground."

"I have him on a leash," Parker said. "He's been my negotiator up to this point. No gunplay. He set up this meeting this morning."

"Maybe it's time to cut that leash?" White said.

"Gentlemen, please," Grover said. "Remember that I represent the territorial governor at this table."

"I wasn't suggesting a shooting," White said. "But it may be time to throw a scare into these farmers to wake them up."

"I'll speak to Cord tonight," Parker said. "I'll ask him to sit in on that vote Johansen and the other farmers have so I get the news before Monday."

"All right, but no gunplay," Grover cautioned.

"How is the hotel here?" White said. "I could use a steak."

# THIRTY-FIVE

James was surprised to see Cord sitting under a tree in the shade several miles out of town. Cord's horse was eating grass in a field behind him.

James slowed the wagon to a stop and looked at Cord.

"What are you doing?" James said.

"Waiting on you."

"Why?"

"I was uninvited from the meeting," Cord said. "Thought you might fill me in before Parker does."

"What's in the sack?" James said.

Beside Cord's right leg was a white sack tied with a rope.

"Cold beer in glass bottles," Cord said. "Want one?"

James set the brake and climbed down from the buckboard. "Could use one," he said.

Cord opened the sack and removed two bottles of beer. The corks were sealed with wax, and he yanked the corks out and handed one bottle to James.

James slid down next to Cord in the shade.

Both men sipped.

"Cold," James said. "You got ice?"

Cord shook his head. "Old Indian trick," he said. "Put them in a sack, tie a rope around it and toss it into a stream or river. The bottles will stay as cool as the bottom of the water."

"Good trick," James said.

Cord rolled a cigarette. "So what went on?" he said.

159

"Parker's upped the stakes to five thousand a farm to buy us out," James said.

"I knew he would," Cord said. "So what now? Are you having any?"

"I'm not, but some of the others might," James said. "We'll put it to another vote and see."

"I figured," Cord said.

"Where do you stand?" James said.

"Are you asking if I'll draw down on the farmers?" Cord said.

"Straight up," James said.

"I won't draw down on anybody without just cause," Cord said. "So don't give me any."

"That's plain enough."

"So when will you have the other vote?"

"Sunday morning if everyone is agreeable."

"Same place?"

"I expect so."

"I'll see you then."

James sipped beer and nodded. "You've seen Parker's kind before?"

"Many times."

"What make a man like him tick?" James said. "What does he need to satisfy himself?"

Cord drew in on the cigarette and slowly let the smoke out. "Everything," he said.

Teasel found Parker in his office in town late in the afternoon.

"Mr. Parker, I can't find John anywhere," Teasel said. "Not at the ranch, the saloon or even the whorehouse."

"Did you see him ride out of town?"

"No, and I can't find anybody who did."

"He was pretty steamed after the meeting," Parker said.

"Maybe he took a ride up to Casper or Black Rock to let loose and cool off."

"Maybe," Teasel said. "Want me to send some of the boys to check?"

"No," Parker said. "I do have a ranch to run. He'll turn up drunk or sober and I'll deal with him then."

"Five thousand dollars, James," Sarah said. "Parker must be desperate to offer that kind of money."

"Would we be rich, Pa?" Seth said.

"Not as rich as this land we own," James said.

"Seth, go do your chores," Sarah said.

"But, Ma."

"*But Ma* me one more time, and I'll take a switch to your bottom," Sarah said.

"Yes, Ma."

Sarah waited for Seth to leave the house and then she said, "James, are you considering Parker's offer?"

"I wasn't."

"Maybe we should?"

"Sarah, this is our home," James said. "We built this place from the bottom up. We just can't hand it over to Parker after the sweat and blood we put into building it."

"We could buy a bigger place near a real town," Sarah said. "One with a church and a school."

"We'll have a school and a church here one day," James said. "Wait and see."

"And if while we are waiting, you are killed by Parker's men, what happens to your wife and son?"

"I understand how you feel, hon, I do," James said. "But what kind of example would I set for Seth if I cut and run at the first sign of trouble? Besides, this has gone beyond one man's greed. One man doesn't have the right to tell another

161

where and how he can live. Not in this country, by God. No sir."

"All right, James," Sarah said. "Go see to Seth while I start supper."

# Thirty-Six

Mal and Keri Jones were sound asleep when the sounds of thunder woke Mal with a start. Earlier there wasn't even a hint of rain in the night air, so the approaching storm was a bit of a surprise.

Mal listened in the dark for a moment, Keri asleep by his side. Then he bolted from the bed when he realized the sound wasn't thunder at all but the sound of a dozen or more charging horses.

Wearing just his nightshirt and with his feet bare, Mal rushed to the living room, grabbed his Winchester seventy-five rifle and raced out to the porch. The late rising moon was a quarter sliver, but provided enough faint light for Mal to see the dozen or more riders on horseback.

They wore white pillowcases over their heads with holes cut for eyes and mouth and were a frightening sight to behold.

"You men, what do you want?" Mal shouted.

Several men rode their horses through Keri's vegetable garden, stomping and squashing the produce.

Mal raced down the porch steps, waving the Winchester.

"Get out of there!" Mal yelled. "Stop that right now."

"Hey, darkie, where's the watermelon?" a rider on horseback said as he rode the horse through the garden.

"Mal?" Keri shouted from the porch.

"Get in the house, woman!" Mal shouted.

Two riders tossed ropes over fence posts on the corral and

163

rode out and knocked over two sections of fence rails.

"Get off my property or I'll shoot!" Mal yelled.

A rider came close to Mal, and Mal could see the whites of his eyes. "No you won't, old darkie," he said. "But we will. You been warned."

Then the rider turned his horse and led the charge off the farm, and within seconds the entire group of riders had disappeared into the night.

"You ain't pulling up stakes, are you, Mal?" James said.

"No man, Parker or otherwise, is driving me off what's mine," Mal said.

James, Mal and Sarah were on the porch. Seth was not allowed in the conversation and was banished to the barn to do chores.

"Keri and your son weren't hurt?" James said.

"They weren't there to hurt us, just scare us," Mal said. "At least not yet anyways."

"Could you identify any of them?" Sarah said.

"Not with them spook hats they had on," Mal said. "But the one who called me darkie, I recognize his voice. Parker's boy for sure."

"You're sure?" James said.

"I'd recognize his voice blindfolded in the dark."

Sarah looked at Mal. "His hired gun?"

Mal shook his head. "I didn't hear his voice, but I doubt he was there. His kind don't hide their faces in the dark when they come to get you. They look you in the eye so you know it was them."

Sarah tried not to show her relief as she nodded.

"I'll ride back with you and help you fix up that fence," James said.

"Obliged, James."

"Have another cup of coffee first," Sarah said. "James, I'll get your pipe."

Sarah went into the house and returned a moment later with the coffeepot and a pipe and pouch for James. She filled cups and then took the pot back into the house.

James filled his pipe and struck a match.

"Last night I had to explain to my son why they called us darkies," Mal said.

"Maybe we should talk to Smiley?" James said.

"Why? He's bought and paid for by Parker, just like all the others," Mal said.

"After the meeting I could ride over to Casper and send a telegram to the US marshal?" James said.

"Who works for the territorial governor," Mal said.

"Then to Washington to the Grange," James said.

"Maybe," Mal said. "Aw, hell, James, I don't even like watermelon."

About to sip coffee, James looked at Mal and then cracked up laughing. Mal stared at James for a moment and then slowly, he too burst into laughter.

James and Mal were still laughing when Sarah emerged from the house wearing her work clothes.

"What are you doing?" James said.

"Seth and I are going with you," Sarah said.

"Fixing fences is men's work, hon," James said.

"But working in Keri's garden isn't," Sarah said.

"Sarah, Keri can . . . ," Mal said.

"Use our help putting things back together," Sarah said. "James, why are you sitting there? Go hitch up the team."

"You didn't come home last night, boy," Parker said when John entered the two-story ranch house on Parker's ranch.

"I stayed on the north range with some of the boys," John

165

said. "We rode after some strays and by the time we had them, it was dark."

"Teasel didn't know anything about it," Parker said.

"I'm a grown man, Pa," John said. "Besides, you said I should stay on the ranch and work. Now you're complaining because I'm doing what you told me to do?"

"I'm not complaining about work," Parker said. "What if you went out alone and your horse threw you? Teasel is foreman around here, and he gives out the assignments."

"Okay, Pa," John said.

"John, someday this ranch and all that goes with it will be yours, but this is not that day," Parker said. "If you make trouble and delay what I've put into motion, it will not sit well for your future. Do you understand me, son?"

"Perfectly."

By late afternoon, James and Mal had the fences repaired, and Sarah and Keri had salvaged half of Keri's third-of-an-acre garden.

"Stay to supper," Keri said. "It won't take me long to get things ready."

"Us long," Sarah said. She looked at James. "Go find your son and tell him to wash at the pump."

"As soon as the farmers are finished with their vote, I want you to ride into town and tell me the result immediately," Parker said.

Cord looked around Parker's town office, at the expensive desk and furniture, the framed map of the territory, which highlighted Parker's ranch with a red boundary. All of the fourteen farms combined would fit inside one of Parker's grazing ranges.

"One, maybe two will go for it," Cord said. "What then?"

166

"My plan is simple but effective and involves no gunplay, unless it's in self-defense," Parker said. "No farmer will be allowed to ship their harvest by my freight line to Medicine Bow to the railroad. It's a long way to Medicine Bow by cart, and a lot can happen on the trail. Tobey's general store will not sell to any farmer on credit, and that includes seeds. If we hit drought they won't be allowed to bring their water barrels to any creek, river or watering hole on my land to irrigate. The Cattlemen's Association will block and delay any legal action taken by the Grange in court. It will take years to sort through it all. In short, I will starve out any farmer who rejects my offer to buy."

"And me?" Cord said.

"You will supervise this entire operation for me, enforce what I need enforced and protect my general interests from any farmer stupid enough to try gunplay," Parker said. "In return, when this is over, you will receive two hundred and fifty of my prime herd, plus four young bulls. When you retire to California, you will be set for life. It's a sweet deal, Cord, for very little work."

Cord nodded. "I'll see you Sunday afternoon."

# Thirty-Seven

"It's no use talking, James," Boyle said. "My mind is set. I'm taking Parker's offer and pulling up stakes."

"If you do that, Parker wins," James said.

"Then he wins," Boyle said. "But so do I. I'm forty-five years old, James. I'm tired of busting my back to scratch out a living. With five thousand dollars, I can move my family west to California and start a new life and not worry about drought, failing crops and surviving winter without food and money. I'm sorry, James, but that's how it is for me and my family."

James looked around at the other farmers gathered at the Jones farm. Most of the wives, including Sarah, had stayed home.

"Anybody else feel the same?" James said.

"I'm leaning that way," Hogan said. "It just don't make sense anymore to try and scratch out a living in the dirt and fight a man like Parker at the same time. I can move my family west to California or east to Ohio where they welcome farmers and don't shoot at them."

"Anybody else pulling out?" James said.

"We're staying, but just until the shooting starts," Sanders said. "I have my wife and daughters to think about, and I'm no gunman."

"Nobody here is a gunman," James said. "And I understand and share your concerns, but one man shouldn't be allowed to tell another where he can live and how to make a living."

"But he is," Boyle said. "And that's just how things are."

"I guess there is nothing more to say," James said. He looked at Cord, who was standing beside his horse. "Two for Parker's offer, twelve against."

Cord nodded, mounted his horse and slowly rode off the Jones farm and veered onto the road.

"Does anybody have anything else to add?" James said.

"It's going to be difficult," Uggla said. "Especially if Parker has our credit cut off at Tobey's and we have to haul our grain to the railroad, but I agree with James. This is free country, and one man shouldn't be able to tell another where to live."

"Monday morning I'll ride into town and tell Parker our decision," James said.

From the west field of the Jones farm, a dozen or more riders were riding in a tight formation. Their faces were covered in white hoods.

The sound of thundering hooves turned the group of farmers around.

"Not again," Mal said. "Not this time."

Mal raced to his house and ran up the steps.

Before James or anyone else could reach their wagons, the riders arrived with guns drawn. Bullets flew, striking the ground, wagons, and the side of the house.

"You men clear out!" James shouted. "This is private property! You hear!"

A rider fired a shot at his feet and James backed up.

Mal ran down his porch steps with his Winchester.

"Get off my land," Mal said.

A rider raced by Mal and struck him in the face with his pistol.

"Mal!" James yelled as Mal hit the ground.

On the porch, Keri screamed.

James and Uggla ran to Mal. James grabbed Mal's Winchester.

"Get him on the porch," James said.

A rider jumped his horse beside James and knocked James to the ground. The rider tossed a rope around James, looped his end around the saddle horn and dragged James through Keri's vegetable garden.

"Stop this, you men! Stop this at once!" Uggla yelled.

Bullets whizzed by Uggla, and he shielded Mal with his body.

The rider dragging James through the garden turned the horse to drag him down the other end.

Suddenly Cord raced in from the road, turned at the garden and in one swoop jumped from his horse and knocked the rider dragging James to the ground.

Cord stood over the rider, grabbed his gun and flung it away. Then Cord yanked the rider to his feet and pulled off the hood.

Cord was not surprised to see the rider was John Parker.

"Father or no father, you asked for this you stupid bastard," Cord said.

Cord punched John in the face, knocking him to the ground. Immediately, Cord pulled John to his feet and backhanded him several times and then punched him again. John fell backward to the ground.

The riders and farmers fell silent as they watched Cord dismantle John.

"Get up, boy," Cord said.

Dazed, hurt, John looked up at Cord.

Cord grabbed John by the shirt.

"I said, get up," Cord said.

Cord lifted John by the shirt and flung him four feet like a rag doll.

"Too many times I've met too many stupid men in my life," Cord said as he kicked John in the ribs. "And they always wind up like you."

Cord kicked John six or seven times in the ribs and stomach.

"No more brains than a wild dog," Cord said.

Cord knelt down and grabbed John's left boot, pulled it off and then the right boot. Cord stood and took hold of John's shirt and pulled on it until it ripped. Then Cord tore it from John's chest, leaving him in his undershirt.

John rolled over and tried to crawl away on his belly, but Cord grabbed John's pants legs and pulled him backward.

"Stop it!" John yelled. "My father—"

"Ain't here," Cord said and ripped the pants right off John, leaving him in his long underwear.

Cord flung the pants away, leaving John on his belly in the dirt.

Then Cord turned and ignored the silent riders as he walked to James. Uggla was kneeling down beside James and he looked at Cord.

"How is he?" Cord said.

"He needs a doctor," Uggla said.

"You men get him on my horse," Cord said. "And somebody ride out and tell his wife he'll be in town."

In the vegetable garden, John crawled to his gun and grabbed it. He cocked it and screamed, "You son of a bitch," and pulled the trigger.

Cord grabbed his .44 revolver just as John's bullet tore into the back of his lower left abdomen. He ignored the bullet wound, spun and cocked and shot John once through the heart.

Nobody moved or made a sound.

Cord holstered the .44.

"You men in the spook hats, you go right now," Cord said.

The riders took off onto the road.

With blood running down his side, Cord looked at Uggla. "Get him on my horse. Tie a rope around his hands and my horse's neck."

"You're shot," Uggla said.

171

"I know I'm shot," Cord said. "Do what I said."

Uggla and Hogan lifted James and placed him on Cord's horse. They used a short rope and tied James in place.

"I'll send the sheriff out to pick up the body," Cord said. "You men best stay put until he arrives."

Cord mounted his horse behind James. Without a word he turned his horse and raced off toward town.

# Thirty-Eight

"He has four busted ribs, a dislocated right shoulder and a concussion," Coy said after he examined James.

"He'll heal?" Cord said.

"He will," Coy said. "He's young and strong, but it will take some time. A month at least before he can do any work."

"I suppose it could have been worse," Cord said.

"About that bullet in your side?" Coy said.

"Went right through," Cord said.

"Let me stitch it up," Coy said.

Cord was shirtless on a table in Coy's back room when Sarah and Seth burst through the curtain.

"James?" Sarah said to Coy as he stitched Cord's side.

"On the table," Coy said. "He's unconscious at the moment. I'll be right there as soon as I finish this stitching."

Sarah and Seth stood over James.

"Mr. Uggla said Parker's son did this," Sarah said. "Why?"

"Meanness. Stupidity. Trying to please his father," Coy said. "If it's any consolation to you, Cord shot and killed him."

"Parker's son?" Sarah said.

"He left me no choice," Cord said. "He shot me in the back. I wasn't about to let him do it again."

"You're done," Coy said to Cord. "Now don't go doing anything to rip those stitches open, and I'll remove them in a week. I'll give you some bandages so you can change them every day. It's important to keep them clean and dry."

Cord stood up, lifted his shirt off the chair and walked to Sarah and Seth.

Sarah looked at the wound on Cord's left lower abdomen. "John Parker did that?" she said.

"He paid for it," Cord said.

Coy walked to the table. "I need to keep James here a few days," he said. "He can't be moved because of the busted ribs, but I want to keep an eye on his concussion."

"What's that?" Seth said.

"Where the horse kicked him," Coy explained. "Put a bad bruise on his head."

Cord slipped on his shirt, buttoned it and tucked it in. "I expect Parker will be wanting to talk to me," he said.

Sarah looked at Cord. "You're in no condition to . . ."

"I'm fine," Cord said. "I'll be back later to check on James."

Parker was about to get into his wagon with Teasel and ride into town to meet with Cord when Sheriff Smiley and his deputies rode in with a body slung over a horse.

Even from a distance Parker recognized the horse as belonging to his son.

Even from a distance Parker recognized the dead body over the horse as that of his son.

"You arrest Cord right now, Sheriff," Parker said from his desk in the den. "And bring him here to me."

"Arrest a man for killing the man that just shot him in the back in front of more than twenty witnesses?" Smiley said. "That won't sit well with nobody, Mr. Parker, least of all me."

"I don't give a goddamn what sits well with you, you stupid oaf. Nobody murders my son and gets away with it," Parker said.

"No, sir," Smiley said. "You can have my badge, but I won't be part of a lynching."

"Get out!" Parker shouted.

Smiley turned and left the office.

As Smiley left, Teasel walked in.

"I found the men who did the . . . rode out there with John," Teasel said.

"Fire them," Parker said. "All of them."

"Yes, sir."

"Then you and I and some of the men will ride to town and find Cord," Parker said.

"Mr. Parker, can I suggest something?" Teasel said.

"What?"

"Wait until after tomorrow, until after you meet with the lieutenant governor and Mr. White," Teasel said. "Get them on your side in this, and they might convince a federal judge to issue a warrant for Cord and send a marshal."

"You're right, of course," Parker said. "I need to stay clearheaded on this. Do you know the place where my wife is buried?"

"I do."

"Have some of the men dig a grave," Parker said. "My son deserves a proper burial. We'll gather the men at dawn and read from the good book."

"Yes, sir."

Cord was at the livery stable at the end of the street where he was about to saddle his horse when Sheriff Smiley and his two deputies rode by.

Cord watched them ride to the sheriff's office, where they dismounted and entered the office.

Cord decided Parker could wait and walked to the office,

opened the door, walked in and looked at Smiley behind his desk.

"I was hoping you rode out and kept going," Smiley said.

"Why would I do that?" Cord said.

"To keep from getting lynched, for one thing," Smiley said.

"What's the other thing?" Cord said.

"Having your neck stretched isn't reason enough?" Smiley said.

Cord looked at the coffeepot on the woodstove. "Is anything in there?"

Smiley nodded to a deputy who filled a cup and gave it to Cord.

"Thanks," Cord said and took a chair facing the desk.

"If I was you, I'd start riding and not stop until I saw the ocean," Smiley said.

"John Parker shot me in the back," Cord said. "James Johansen is over at Coy's place with busted ribs and a concussion after being roped by John Parker and dragged by his horse. Do they hang a man around here for getting shot in the back?"

"Parker has thirty-five or forty hands on his spread," Smiley said. "He'll have every last one of them on the warpath after you by this time tomorrow. I won't be able to stop him once they pick you out a tree."

"I'm not much for running when I'm in the right," Cord said. "Parker will be in town tomorrow, and I'll see him then."

"I talked to everyone at the Jones place," Smiley said. "By all accounts John Parker got exactly what he deserved, so I have no cause to hold you in my jail. I wish I did for your own protection."

Cord stared at Smiley. "If Parker and his men ride in and I'm in your jail and they demand you turn me over to them, we both know exactly what you'll do."

Smiley lowered his eyes and looked at the desk.

Cord stood up. "Thanks for the coffee," he said.

Sarah came out of Coy's barbershop, spotted Cord walking to the livery and caught up to him.

"Mr. Cord," she said.

Cord stopped and turned around. "How is he?"

"Awake for a bit," Sarah said. "Mr. Coy said he can't be moved because of the ribs, but he thinks the concussion isn't as bad as he first thought."

"That's good."

"I don't know what to say," Sarah said.

"Then say nothing," Cord said.

"Will you be leaving?"

"Not until I set a few things straight with Parker."

"He'll have you killed."

"I have to tend to my horse."

"Wait."

Cord looked at Sarah.

"I think maybe you should come home with me . . . and Seth," Sarah said. "Stay the night in the barn. If Mr. Parker's men are out looking for you, that's the last place they will look."

"I don't think that would be proper," Cord said.

"Oh, hang proper," Sarah said. "You saved my husband's life and probably a few others today. I don't think anybody cares about proper."

"All right, I'll ride out to your place later," Cord said. "I have a few things to tend to first."

"Be careful," Sarah cautioned. "Parker owns this entire town."

Cord nodded. "There's a lot of that going on these days," he said.

# THIRTY-NINE

Cord found White and Grover eating steaks in the hotel dining room. He didn't wait for an invitation, but pulled out a chair and took a seat.

"I'm Cord," he said. "Which one of you is which?"

"Paul Grover, lieutenant governor, and this is Mr. White of the Cattlemen's Association," Grover said. "What can we do for you, Mr. Cord?"

"I've just killed Parker's son to prevent him from killing James Johansen and maybe a few other farmers who were having a meeting," Cord said. "John Parker and a dozen or so of Parker's hands rode in and shot up the farm belonging to the Jones family. They wore masks to cover their faces. The Parker boy shot me in the back and would have done it again, so I killed him."

"I see," Grover said.

"The sheriff ain't worth spit in this town, so when Parker takes the law into his own hands, nobody is going to stop him," Cord said.

"Wyoming is a territory, but we do have laws, Mr. Cord," Grover said. "A US marshal can be here in ten days."

"I have a better idea," Cord said. "You two finish your steaks, then you leave town and don't stop until you're home."

"Now why would we do that?" White said.

"Because if you don't, I will come to your hotel rooms and kill you both in your sleep, that's why you will do that," Cord said.

Grover and White stared at Cord as if they misunderstood his words.

Finally Grover said, "Is this some sort of joke?"

"Stick around and find out," Cord said.

"You're threatening the lieutenant governor of this territory," Grover said.

"And if you don't make it back, the governor will just appoint another one," Cord said. "Your business with Parker is concluded. You have no good reason to stick around town unless you think being dead is a good reason. I'll be on the street watching for you to ride out. Don't disappoint me."

An hour later, Cord sat in a chair in front of the livery stables with a cup of coffee and a rolled cigarette and watched as Grover and White rode out of town in a buggy. They kept their eyes straight ahead and didn't look at Cord as they rode past him.

Once they were out of town and on the road north, Cord stood up and saddled his horse.

It was dark by the time he reached the Johansen farm.

"Mr. Coy said my pa will be all right," Seth said at the dinner table. "He can come home in a few days when his busted ribs don't hurt so bad."

"Badly, Seth," Sarah said. "Hurt so badly. Remember your grammar."

"Yes, Ma," Seth said.

"That was a fine dinner," Cord said.

"I made a pot of coffee," Sarah said. "We'll have some on the porch. Seth, clear the table and then join us."

"Yes, Ma," Seth said.

★ ★ ★ ★ ★

Cord rolled a cigarette as he and Sarah drank coffee on the porch.

"What happens now?" Sarah said. "Now that his son is dead, will Parker still want to buy out the farms?"

"My guess is he will start a range war and take the farms by force," Cord said. "He's angry and bitter and he believes that since he was here first, he's entitled to it all."

"And he's willing to start a war and kill to get it?" Sarah said.

"Count on it," Cord said.

"And you?"

"You might say I'm stuck in the middle."

"You could just ride out and forget this place."

"I could."

Seth opened the door and stepped out onto the porch and stood beside Sarah.

"I finished cleaning up, Ma," Seth said.

"Sit with Mr. Cord while I go get a pan of water and some bandages," Sarah said.

"No need," Cord said.

"I'll be right back," Sarah said. "Seth, you watch him."

Seth grinned. "Yes, Ma."

Sarah went into the house and Seth took a chair.

"Your ma has a stubborn streak in her," Cord said.

Seth leaned in close to Cord. "Promise you won't say nothing to my pa when he gets home?" he whispered.

"I can't promise unless I know what I'm promising," Cord said.

Seth looked at the door to make sure Sarah wasn't coming out and then he said, "Sometimes I think my ma is the boss around here. My pa pretends like he is, but I think it's my ma."

"I'll tell you a secret you best learn now," Cord whispered. "Women are always in charge. Men just pretend to be."

Seth sat back in his chair and looked at Cord in disbelief.

"It's true," Cord said.

The door opened and Sarah carried out a basin of water and set it on the porch floor.

"Seth, turn the lantern on high," she said and quickly went back inside.

Seth stood to reach the hanging lantern and turned the dial to enlarge the flame.

Sarah returned with gauze, a towel and a bottle of rubbing alcohol.

"Shirt off, Mr. Cord," Sarah said.

Cord looked at Seth, winked and stood up. He opened the buttons on his shirt and removed it.

"Under the light," Sarah said.

Cord moved closer to the lantern.

"Seth, peel off the bandage," Sarah said.

Seth cautiously reached for the bandage on Cord's left abdomen. "It might hurt," he said as he pulled the bandage away from Cord's skin.

"Ouch," Cord cried.

"Sorry," Seth said.

Sarah poured alcohol onto a piece of gauze and dabbed it on the wound.

"Ah!" Cord said.

"Don't be such a baby, Mr. Cord," Sarah said.

Seth grinned and said, "I know how it feels."

"Other side," Sarah said.

Cord turned and Sarah washed the back side of the wound.

"Very little leaking," Sarah said as she wiped blood with a wet towel. "Mr. Coy did a fine job with the stitches."

"I forgot to pay him," Cord said. "I must remember to do that."

Sarah poured alcohol on the stitches and then wrapped clean

gauze on the wounds, being careful not to press too hard.

"It will probably leak a bit from sleeping on them," Sarah said. "I'll change them before you leave in the morning."

Cord reached for his shirt and slipped it on. "Don't go into town," he said. "I'll check on your husband and when he's fit enough, I'll bring him home."

"Mr. Parker doesn't frighten me," Sarah said.

"I didn't say he did," Cord said.

Sarah nodded. "All right," she said. "Seth, get the extra pillow and then take Mr. Cord to the barn and say good night."

"Be right back," Seth said and dashed into the house.

Cord looked at Sarah. After a moment, she blushed and turned away from him.

"Don't look at me that way," Sarah said.

"What way is that?"

"Like you . . ."

Seth opened the door and stepped out with a pillow in his arms.

"I made up a place in the barn when Ma said you were coming," Seth said. "I'll show you."

Cord nodded to Sarah. "Good night," he said.

"Be mindful of the stitches," Sarah said. "You don't want to open them in your sleep."

Sarah watched Cord and Seth walk to the barn. Once they were inside, a lantern was lit, and after a few minutes Seth returned to the house.

"Did Mr. Cord get settled in all right?" Sarah said.

"Yes, Ma," Seth said.

"Good, now it's your turn," Sarah said.

Before dawn Seth entered the barn as silently as possible in case Cord was still asleep. Ma had already started breakfast, and he needed to get his chores done before she was finished or eat it cold.

Carefully, the way Pa showed him, Seth withdrew a wood match from the tinderbox on the shelf beside the lantern, struck the match and lit the wick.

Cord was gone and so was his horse.

Seth raced back to the house.

"Ma, he's gone," Seth said. "Mr. Cord left and didn't say good-bye."

Sarah, mixing dough in a bowl, looked at Seth.

"Did he take his bedroll?" Sarah said.

"No, no, he did not."

"Then he'll be back," Sarah said. "Go do your chores."

# FORTY

Cord had breakfast at the Brooks Hotel dining room shortly after they opened at six thirty in the morning.

A few dusty trail hands and cowboys came in shortly after Cord, but the morning rush didn't start until seven.

After eating, Cord took a cup of coffee to the hotel porch where he sat, rolled a cigarette and watched the street.

After an hour or so, Cord returned to the dining room to refill his cup and then returned to the porch. He rolled and smoked another cigarette and spotted Sheriff Smiley coming out of the jail.

Smiley walked directly to the hotel and joined Cord on the porch.

"I saw you sitting here," Smiley said. "I thought you should know Parker buried his son this morning at dawn. I was there. He's on his way to town right now to meet with the lieutenant governor and Ed White."

Cord sipped from his cup and stared at Smiley.

"You know what's going to happen around here. When it does happen, you and your deputies are going to sit back and watch," Cord said.

"Mister, don't tell me how to do my job," Smiley said.

"No need," Cord said. "You have Parker for that."

"Why don't you clear on out?" Smiley said. "You don't work for Parker anymore. You got no stake in this town or what happens here."

"Not until Parker and me get a few things straight," Cord said.

Smiley looked down the street.

"Now is your chance," Smiley said.

A buggy driven by Teasel arrived at Parker's office at the end of the street. In the passenger seat, Parker climbed down and walked to his office door and opened it with a key.

Teasel dismounted and followed Parker inside.

"What are you going to do?" Smiley said.

Cord slowly stood up.

"Hide and watch," Cord said as he walked down to the street.

Sarah stirred the boiling cauldron that was full of clothes and looked at Seth.

"If you can do it without prying, see if Mr. Cord has some dirty shirts that could use washing," Sarah said.

Seth ran from the side of the house to the barn where Cord left his saddlebags beside the pillow. Carefully, Seth went through the twin bags and removed three shirts and one set of long underwear. He carried the bundle of clothes to the boiling cauldron.

Sarah removed the clothes from inside the cauldron using a long stick and hung them on a line between two posts and nodded to Seth.

Seth gently tossed in Cord's clothes, and Sarah pushed them to the bottom of the boiling water with the stick.

"Could use some more firewood," Sarah said.

Seth grabbed two logs from the stack beside the caldron and added them to the fire beneath the black pot. Hung from a metal tripod, the cauldron was easy to tip if you weren't careful.

Behind Sarah was a basin full of soapy water for washing and another for rinsing once the clothes were boiled. She removed the clothes from the line and put them into the basin full of soapy water.

"Mr. Cord will be surprised to find his shirts clean," Seth said.

"Once we're done here, it's time for schoolwork," Sarah said.

"Aw, Ma," Seth said.

"I suppose we could skip schoolwork today and pack a picnic lunch," Sarah said. "If your father were here, I'm sure he'd agree."

"I'll go get the basket," Seth said.

When Cord opened the door to Parker's town office, the reactions of Parker at his desk and Teasel standing against the wall were shock and disbelief.

As Cord walked to the desk, Teasel moved against the wall and Cord held out his right hand.

"Stay as you are," Cord said to Teasel. "Or die as you are."

Parker opened the middle drawer of his desk and stuck his hand inside.

Cord pulled the .38 from the shoulder rig, cocked and aimed it at Parker.

"Don't give me a reason," Cord said.

Parker closed the drawer and sat back in the chair.

"You murdered my son," Parker said. "He was barely a man."

"Your son shot me in the back," Cord said.

"You could have wounded him," Parker said.

"He was about to shoot me again," Cord said. "He left me no choice."

"What is it you want?" Parker said. "You have to be smart enough to know you no longer work for me."

"I wanted to tell you that before your son showed up with his friends in their spook hats, I had convinced two, maybe three farmers to take your deal," Cord said. "Your son ruined it for you. I doubt they will be so inclined today after what happened.

186

I also wanted to tell you that Grover and White have left town rather suddenly."

"We have a meeting," Parker said.

"It's been canceled."

Parker glared at Cord.

"Leave them alone, Parker," Cord said. "Don't start a range war over land you don't need. There's been enough killing already."

"I don't figure this, gunfighter," Parker said. "What do you care who gets killed so long as you get paid?"

"You read me wrong, Parker," Cord said.

"I guess I did," Parker said. "I guess even a hired gun can have a soft spot for a pretty woman, and Sarah Johansen is one pretty woman. Ain't that right?"

Cord moved so quickly Parker didn't have time to react as Cord smacked him in the face with the .38.

"You filthy-minded old man. I should kill you right now," Cord said.

Blood ran down Parker's nose and lip. He seemed to ignore it as he looked at Cord with hatred.

"Leave town, gunfighter," Parker said. "Leave Wyoming. If you don't, I will have you killed and your body dragged across Main Street in back of my buggy."

"I'll say this one more time," Cord said. "Leave these farmers be and make do with all the wealth you now have, or I promise you that you will see hell."

Holding the .38 aimed at Parker, Cord backed up to the door, opened it and walked out to the street.

"I'm obliged to you for saving my life," James said. "Coy told me what you did; Uggla and Mal Jones told me the same."

"How do you feel?" Cord said.

187

"Like I have four broken ribs and a dislocated shoulder," James said.

Cord turned and looked at Coy.

"Can he travel?" Cord said.

"Day after tomorrow if you pad his wagon with a thick bed of hay and some blankets," Coy said. "I'll ride with him to see nothing happens."

"I'm all right," James said.

"Yeah? Let me see you get out of that bed under your own steam," Coy said.

James moved as if to sit up and collapsed against the pillow in obvious pain.

"I'll be back day after tomorrow with the wagon," Cord said.

Parker drank two fingers of rye whiskey in one quick gulp and then refilled the glass and sat back in his chair.

"Mr. Parker, are you all right?" Teasel said.

"My son is dead," Parker said. "He was shot down and murdered like a rabid dog by filthy scum."

"Yes, sir, I know."

"He never even got to be a man."

Parker downed the second glass of rye whiskey and looked at Teasel.

"Mr. Parker, are you all right?" Teasel said.

"I want to go home," Parker said.

"There was no need to do this," Cord said when Sarah and Seth presented him with clean, dry shirts and long underwear.

"I think we owe you more than some clean laundry," Sarah said.

"Ma and me made a picnic lunch for us," Seth said. "We'll go down by the creek, is that okay?"

"That's fine with me," Cord said.

"Did Mr. Coy check your stitches?" Sarah said.

"No."

"Seth, get the alcohol and bandages."

"Then can we go?" Seth said.

"Yes."

Seth dashed into the house.

"You might as well put a clean shirt to good use," Sarah said.

Cord removed his shirt and hung it over the porch railing.

Sarah looked at the stitches.

"You're leaking," she said.

"It's nothing," Cord said.

Seth returned with bandages and the alcohol. He looked at Cord. "It's bloody."

"Seth, take Mr. Cord around back to the shower," Sarah said. "He might as well wash all of him before I put on clean bandages."

"What's a shower?" Cord said.

"My pa built it," Seth said. "I'll show you."

Seth took Cord by the hand and led him down the steps to the rear of the house where a square wood stall sat under a large barrel on the roof.

"You open the door and get in," Seth explained. "Then you turn that little wheel and the water comes out that spout Pa cut from a watering can. Once you're all wet, turn the water off and use the soap to scrub up, and then you turn the water back on to rinse off. Pa says people back east in places like New York and Boston have them right in the house."

"Your pa built this?" Cord said.

"Except for the spout," Seth said. "He got that from a watering can he got from Mr. Tobey."

Cord opened the door and stepped into the stall.

"I'll get you a towel," Seth said. "Oh, don't forget to take off your pants."

Seth brought two fishing poles to the creek so he and Cord could try their luck after the picnic.

"Your pa should be strong enough to travel in the next two days or so," Cord said. "I spoke to him this morning, and he's raring to come home."

"That sounds like Pa," Seth said.

"He's hurting, though," Cord said. "We have to fix up the wagon so when I ride him home we don't damage his busted ribs."

"How?" Seth said.

"Line the wagon with a bale of hay and blankets," Cord said. "Coy said he would ride in the wagon with him to keep him from getting bounced around."

"Can I go when you bring him home?" Seth said.

"If you go with me, you won't be able to give him a big welcome when I get him home," Cord said.

"I guess," Seth said.

"Seth, why don't you dig along the creek for some worms for the fishing poles while Mr. Cord and I finish our coffee," Sarah said.

"I know just where they are," Seth said.

Seth walked down to the bed of the creek to look for worms.

Cord pulled out his tobacco pouch and rolled a cigarette.

Sarah watched him go through the process of sprinkling tobacco on a paper, rolling it, pinching off the ends and striking a wood match to light the cigarette.

"Why do you hide your obvious breeding?" Sarah said.

"I wasn't aware that I was," Cord said.

Sarah sipped her coffee and studied Cord for a moment. Without his hat on, his long dark hair came to his shoulders.

The beard was sprinkled with specks of gray the same color as his eyes.

He had a way about him that was different from most people. When you stared at him, he never looked away or seemed uncomfortable. That air of confidence caused you to avert your eyes and, in Sarah's case, to blush.

She was blushing now. She knew it and couldn't stop it from happening. Her only option was to look away.

"Mr. Cord, I need something to dig with," Seth said from the creek bed.

"Be right there," Cord said and stood up.

As he pulled the massive bayonet from his belt and walked down to the creek, Sarah whispered, "Damn you."

"I have no son," Parker said, slurring his words. "No heir to leave my ranch to when I go."

Teasel stood before Parker's desk in the den of Parker's ranch home. Parker drank nearly the entire bottle of rye on the trip home and had started on a second bottle from the bar in the den.

"Mr. Parker, can I get you some food?" Teasel said.

"I don't want food," Parker said. "Sit down and listen to me."

Teasel took a chair and looked at Parker.

"How long you been with me?" Parker said.

"About ten years."

"They call that a decade."

"I know," Teasel said, softly.

"My son is gone and I am alone," Parker said.

"Mr. Parker, the cook can . . ."

"Listen to me, listen to me," Parker said. "I'm alone in this now. I can't count on the governor or anybody else. I got to do this myself."

"Do what, Mr. Parker?" Teasel said.

"My son was no good. I know that," Parker said. He gulped rye from his glass. "But he was all I had."

"He's at rest now, Mr. Parker."

Parker sat up straight and looked at Teasel through bloodshot eyes. "You help me win this, drive these farmers out, and I will make you a full partner in my ranch and my heir when I'm gone."

Teasel was stunned at the offer.

"I'm . . . I'm not your blood," Teasel said.

"You're more of a son to me than John ever was," Parker said.

"What do you want me to do?" Teasel said.

"Exactly what I tell you," Parker said. "Tell the cook to fix us something to eat and we'll discuss things."

# FORTY-ONE

Teasel sat in a chair on the porch of the bunkhouse with a cup of coffee and watched the moon slowly rise above the tree line.

The sky was clear, a million stars twinkled overhead and the moon would be full and bright in an hour or so once it rose to greet the stars.

Four men were on night watch, two in the tower, two on foot. As the moon slowly bathed the ground in its pale light, he could see the faint outlines of the men in the tower.

The bunkhouse was dark and quiet. Most of the hands were on the drive to move the massive herd from the west range to the north range. They would be gone another thirty-six hours or so.

A half dozen hands stayed behind for fence work and strays. They were asleep in their bunks.

Which was where he should be if he had an ounce of sense, but he knew sleep was still hours away from now.

He had to get his mind around what Mr. Parker wanted and offered him in return for helping Parker get it.

Could he drive the farmers out, burn their crops and homes for the sake of wealth and power?

Was he that kind of man?

Teasel sipped his coffee and then rolled a cigarette.

Maybe if he did what Mr. Parker asked, instead of bringing in another hired gun, nobody had to die?

There was some redemption in that thought.

If he handled things instead of another man like Cord, bloodshed might be avoided.

And maybe, when it was over, he would still own a tiny piece of his soul?

# FORTY-TWO

The night breeze was cool on her face. Sarah sat on the porch wearing just her nightshirt and sipped cold milk from a glass.

It was after eleven and Seth had been asleep for hours.

The sounds of night were all around her.

Crickets, owls, the chickens squawking in their sleep, the horses in the corral making night noises.

She was alone and surrounded by sound.

The moon was full and high, and she didn't need to light the lantern to see the barn, chicken house and corral.

The barn was dark.

Cord was asleep, probably.

As she should be.

And that is exactly what she would be as soon as she finished her milk.

Sarah set the glass of milk on the porch railing.

Go in the house and get into bed and go to sleep.

And not stir until morning.

Sarah stood from the chair and slowly walked down the porch steps.

Barefoot, she walked across the yard to the barn.

Don't be a fool, she told herself. Don't touch that door.

And reached for the barn door.

Do not go in there under any circumstances.

Sarah slowly cracked open the barn door. Soft moonlight filtered over her shoulder to the barn floor.

Turn around. Turn around and leave right now.

Sarah entered the barn and softly closed the door.

Cord was in his bedroll.

"Who is it?" he said in his raspy voice.

"Sarah," she said. "I came to check your stitches."

Cord stood up, shirtless, his chest reflecting soft moonlight coming in through the window.

"No, you didn't," he said.

"No, I didn't," Sarah agreed.

"Come closer into the moonlight," Cord said.

Sarah walked to Cord and stood looking up at him.

"Why did you come in here?" Cord said.

With her eyes locked on Cord's, Sarah slowly pulled the nightshirt over her head to reveal that she wore nothing underneath.

Cord looked at her in the pale moonlight.

"Lord," he said.

Snuggled inside his bedroll, Sarah placed her face on Cord's chest and closed her eyes for a moment.

She wanted to stay right there and sleep until morning, but she knew she couldn't, that she had to be dressed and making breakfast for Seth before he woke up, as was the usual.

She opened her eyes.

"I need to know about the man I betrayed my husband for," Sarah said.

"I'm not much for talking about myself," Cord said.

"If nothing else, you owe me that," Sarah said.

Cord wrapped his arm around her. "How about I start from sixty-three?"

"Just so long as you tell me something," Sarah said.

"I was fifteen in sixty-three," Cord said. "My folks had a three-hundred-acre spread in west Missouri not far from the breaks. We didn't think the war would touch us, but one fine afternoon when I was in the field the Confederate Raiders came calling. They took what they needed, shot and killed my father, raped my mother and then killed her and my little brother, who was all of eleven at the time. I didn't know what was happening until I saw the smoke from my house burning down. I ran as fast as I could, but by the time I got there, the house and barn were gone. I knew they raped my mother because I found her dress slung over a fence post near the corral."

Sarah felt her eyes start to mist, and she choked back tears.

"Go on," she said.

"I went north to Chicago to find a Yankee recruiting station and joined the Union army," Cord said. "I was big for my age and told them I was eighteen, and they were happy to have me. I had five dollars in my pocket and the fifty-caliber Plains rifle my father gave me for my fourteenth birthday. When they saw in training I could hit the eye out of a bird at a thousand yards, they put me in a special squad. Snipers, they called us. I spent the war killing as many Rebs as possible from a distance. On Sherman's March to the Sea, my squad went ahead and killed everything that moved or crawled. To make way for the general."

"And after the war?"

"I had nowhere to go and nobody to go to, so I stayed and went to West Point," Cord said. "In sixty-seven, they sent me west as a second lieutenant. My mission was to help with the pacification of the Indians to allow the railroad to connect east to west. Do you know what pacification means?"

"Yes," Sarah said in a whisper.

"By seventy, I had a stomach full of killing. When my time was up, I left the army and stayed west," Cord said.

"I don't understand," Sarah said. "If you had a stomach full of killing, why do you sell your gun to people like Parker?"

"Some people just deserve killing," Cord said. "But mostly I sell my gun out to stop killing. I have a small ranch in California. A few hundred head and fifty horses or so. When I have a big enough herd, I go west and that's the end of it. This would have been my final job, as my fee to settle this was two hundred and fifty head and four bulls. I guess that deal has fallen through."

"Where in California?" Sarah said.

"Thirty miles north of San Diego to the west," Cord said. "It's beautiful country."

"Have you seen the ocean?"

"Twice in my life I have seen the ocean," Cord said. "Once on Sherman's March to the Sea and the other time when I bought my ranch in California. The Pacific is a sight to see when the sun comes up and the water is calm. All I remember about the Atlantic is blood in the water from dead Confederates who tried to make a rush. The waves were pink as they crashed to shore. Arms and legs floating. I've seen enough of the Atlantic Ocean to last me a lifetime."

She had the urge to cry, but Sarah choked it down and pressed her face to Cord's.

"I was hoping to settle this dispute without gunplay," Cord said. "Take my cattle and drive them west and be done with it all. I don't think that's possible now."

Sarah slowly sat up and looked at Cord.

"I don't know what Parker will do now, but I'm sure he will do something, and it won't be good," Cord said.

"I know," Sarah said.

"The best thing you could do right now is move your family out of here before Parker makes his play," Cord said.

"How?" Sarah said. "With James in the back of a wagon. Go where?"

"That old cap-and-ball Navy revolver you showed me, does it work?" Cord said.

"I don't know."

"I'll get you something a little bit newer."

"What about you? What are you going to do in all this?"

"Probably get my fool head blown off," Cord said.

"In that case," Sarah said, and pressed her body hard against his.

# FORTY-THREE

"Are you sure you don't want me to go with you to Casper?" Teasel said as Parker climbed aboard his buggy.

"Quite sure," Parker said. "I'll be back late tomorrow afternoon sometime. Keep the herd moving to the north range and gather up the strays. It's business as usual until I return."

"I'd feel better if at least you took a firearm," Teasel said and placed a Winchester rifle on the seat beside Parker.

"See you late tomorrow," Parker said. He cracked the buggy whip, and the horse broke into a slow trot.

Sarah sat on the porch and snapped open sugar snap peas as she watched Cord chop wood by the woodshed.

Seth stood off to the side with the wooden wheelbarrow and waited for it to fill up before pushing it into the shed to off-load.

Shirtless, as Cord slammed the ax into a thick log the muscles in his shoulders, his arms and back rippled.

Sarah knew that she should have felt a deep shame in her behavior, but instead she wanted to run down there and grab Cord and smother him in her arms.

She didn't.

She continued to snap peas and cast glances his way.

"The shed is almost full," Seth said after returning with the empty wheelbarrow.

"Then we'll fill it and start loading the barn," Cord said.

"That could take all day," Seth said.

"It's going to be weeks, maybe even a month before your pa can swing an ax," Cord said. "You want your ma doing this?"

Seth looked at Sarah on the porch. "No, sir," he said.

"So let's finish this and then go check your fields," Cord said. "I see storm clouds dogging us, and those water barrels in the fields have the lids on them."

"Mr. Cord," Sarah said. "Mind those stitches or you'll pop them."

Cord looked at her.

"Yes, ma'am," he said.

Seth gazed at Cord, amazed that he would so readily obey his ma's commands.

Cord winked. "Remember what I told you," Cord said. "A woman is always the boss."

Cord removed the sixth and final cover from the water barrels in the fields and peered inside. As with the others, it was half full. If the dark clouds gathering produced as much rain as he thought they would, the barrels should be three quarters full by the storm's end.

"Why not just leave the covers off all the time?" Seth said as he and Cord walked the long rows of wheat and corn.

"There is something called evaporation," Cord said. "Know what that is?"

Seth shook his head.

"Ever see a puddle dry up in the sun?"

"Sure."

"Same thing would happen if the barrels weren't covered."

Cord looked at the dark, gray sky.

"We best beat the storm back," Cord said.

★ ★ ★ ★ ★

The first crack of thunder came during supper.

Sarah, on edge all day, flinched at the roaring boom.

"It's all right, Ma," Seth said. "It's just thunder from the storm."

"I know what it is, Seth," Sarah said. "Are the horses in the barn?"

"Yes, Ma, and I covered the chicken coop," Seth said.

Lightning flashed outside the open windows and was quickly followed by another loud thunderclap.

Hard rain started before the clap faded away.

Cord stood up from the table and went to each window to close the shutters.

"Maybe Mr. Cord should sleep in the house tonight, Ma?" Seth said. "He can share my room."

Cord returned to the table.

"No need of that," Cord said. "Besides, me sleeping in the barn may keep the cows and horses from getting jumpy."

"The roof leaks in the barn," Seth said.

"I'm sure Mr. Cord will be just fine," Sarah said, looking at Cord.

Shortly after midnight, when she opened the barn door and stepped inside, Sarah was soaked from the hard rain that showed no sign of letting up.

Just walking the few hundred feet from porch to barn was enough to soak through her robe to her skin.

She closed the door, and her eyes searched for Cord in the dark.

A match lit, followed by a low flame in the lantern beside Cord's bedroll.

"Please tell me to turn around and go back to the house," Sarah said. "Because if you don't, I will stay."

Cord stood up and walked to her. "I want you to stay," he said and gently removed the wet robe.

# Forty-Four

"That should do it," Cord said as he spread blankets over the bale of hay he laid down in the wagon.

"The pillow," Seth said and handed it to Cord.

"If everything goes right I should be back around noon with your pa," Cord said. He looked around for Sarah, but she was nowhere to be found.

"Tell your ma I left," Cord said.

Seth nodded. "She's in the house I think."

Cord climbed aboard the buckboard. He yanked on the reins, and the horses moved forward.

Seth watched until Cord was on the road, and then he went into the house.

Sarah was rolling dough with the heavy rolling pin on the table.

"Mr. Cord left to get Pa," Seth said.

"I heard," Sarah said. "Go to the icehouse and pick out a dozen good apples. I think your father deserves a pie for tonight, don't you?"

Seth grinned and raced out of the house.

Sarah rolled and rolled the dough. Then she suddenly started to shake and violently slammed the rolling pin onto the table.

"Damn you," she said, sat, and started to cry.

Seth returned with his arms loaded with apples. He set them on the table and touched Sarah on the shoulder.

"What's wrong, Ma?" Seth said.

"Nothing. I'm just happy and relieved that your father is coming home."

"Me, too, Ma," Seth said. "But I ain't gonna cry about it."

Sarah looked at Seth, laughed and hugged him. "Let's make that pie," she said.

"I can make it on my own steam on my own two legs," James said when Coy suggested a stretcher.

"Let me see you get out of that bed on your own without passing out from pain and I'll agree," Coy said.

James tried to rise up from the bed and grunted in pain. His face turned red and he flopped back down.

Coy turned to Cord. "We'll need two more men," he said.

"Be right back," Cord said.

Cord entered Tobey's general store and waited for Tobey to ring up a sale of yarn to a local woman in town, then he went to the counter.

"Where do you keep the firearms?" Cord said.

"Out back in a separate room," Tobey said.

"Let me have a look."

Tobey led Cord behind a long curtain to a storeroom.

"That door," Tobey said and used a key to unlock the door.

Lined against the wall were Winchester rifles of several different models. On a counter were Smith & Wesson, Remington and Colt revolvers.

"I'll take the Winchester seventy-five in forty-five and that Colt revolver in forty-five and a case of shells," Cord said.

"How many weapons does one man need?" Tobey said as he looked at Cord's gun belt and shoulder holster.

"Depends on the man," Cord said. "How much?"

"Forty-five dollars, and I toss in the shells for free."

"Obliged."

Cord set the rifle and revolver in the buckboard of the wagon and then walked down the wood sidewalk to the sheriff's office.

Smiley and his deputies were drinking coffee at the desk.

"I can't believe you're still around," Smiley said.

"Need two men to help carry Johansen to the wagon," Cord said.

"Don't jangle him too much," Coy said. "Those ribs are far from healed."

Cord, Tobey and Smiley's two deputies carried James on a wood stretcher from the barbershop to the wagon.

"Is he sleeping?" a deputy said.

"I gave him some morphine for the pain," Coy said. "He'll sleep the trip to his house."

Once James was loaded onto the back of the wagon, Coy took his black doctor's bag in back and sat beside James.

Cord climbed onto the buckboard and started the horses moving.

"Slow and easy," Coy said. "And I do mean slow."

After lunch, Sarah and Seth sat on the porch to wait for the wagon to arrive. Seth spotted the wagon with Coy's horse in tow as it turned off the road, and he jumped from the porch to the ground without hitting one step.

"Pa, Pa!" Seth cried as he raced to meet the wagon.

Sarah stood and watched as Cord lifted Seth to the seat and they rode to the house together.

Coy stepped down from the wagon and met Sarah as she came down the porch steps. "He's full of morphine," Coy said. "I figured it best if he was out for the ride home. Once we get him inside I'll tell you how to care for him."

Alone on the porch, Cord gave Sarah the Winchester and Colt revolver. "That Plains rifle and eighteen-sixty cap and ball aren't much good," he said. "Keep the rifle away from the boy, but keep it handy. The Colt is a good backup to have if things get close."

"You're expecting trouble," Sarah said.

"It's better to be prepared than not," Cord said.

"You're going?" Sarah said.

Cord nodded.

"Where?"

"Not far," Cord said.

Sarah felt her eyes mist up and she turned away.

Seth came out to the porch. "Mr. Coy said Pa will wake up soon," Seth said.

Sarah nodded.

Seth looked at her and then at Cord. "What's wrong?" Seth said.

"Mr. Cord is leaving us," Sarah said.

"Why?" Seth said. "My pa ain't well yet. We need you to stay."

Cord ran his hand through Seth's hair. "I'll see you again," he said.

"But we need you here," Seth said. "My pa needs you and my ma wants you to stay. Tell him, Ma. Tell him you want him to stay."

Sarah looked into Cord's eyes. "Mr. Cord has business elsewhere, Seth. It isn't fair of us to tie him down. I'm sure we'll see him again. Right?"

Cord nodded.

Then he stepped down off the porch, walked to his horse, mounted up and rode off onto the road.

Sarah placed her arm around Seth.

"Let's go see to your father," she said.

# FORTY-FIVE

"How long I been asleep?" James said when he opened his eyes and saw Sarah seated in a chair beside the bed.

"Seven hours, maybe a bit more," Sarah said. "Hungry?"

"I could eat," James said.

"I have stew keeping hot over the fireplace," Sarah said. "Let's see if we can get you to sit up."

Sarah stood and gently placed her arms around his shoulders and, with James pushing and her pulling, they managed to get him into a seated position.

Red-faced and gasping, James said, "That wasn't so bad. I'll be behind the plow in no time."

"Not unless you eat," Sarah said. "I made fresh bread, too. I'll be right back."

Sarah went into the kitchen where Seth was doing math problems in his tablet at the table.

"Your father is awake and hungry," Sarah said. "Let's bring him some food."

Cord stirred the ashes from his campfire to make sure they were out before settling into his bedroll.

He was camped near the creek for the fresh water.

His horse was hobbled close by the bedroll.

The moon was full and bright. A million stars twinkled overhead. It was a perfect night to be alive. He felt as if there was a deep hole in his gut that could never be filled.

He pulled out tobacco pouch and paper, rolled a cigarette and lit it with a wood match.

He should feel guilt at having taken another man's wife, but he didn't. He realized that deep hole in his gut was left by her absence. Only her presence would fill it up.

The thing to do was put her from his mind and concentrate on Parker.

Men like Parker were fueled by more than their wealth, land or power. What really made them tick was their pride, and Parker's was his driving force.

Parker saw himself as above it all and catering to no man. His arrogance wouldn't accept defeat. That meant he would have to react, and there was no telling what his reaction would be.

Gunplay would probably come last, after all else failed.

The trick would be to figure out what the *all else* that came first would be and then anticipate the gunplay.

Most likely negotiations with the farmers were out of the question.

Parker could starve them out by having credit cut off at the bank and general store and make it really tough on them by forcing them to carry their grain by wagon to Medicine Bow to the railroad.

He could dam up the creeks and rivers that ran through his property and dry up them up so water wouldn't flow to the farms.

Whatever Parker finally decided to do, bloodshed was sure to follow.

Cord took a final puff on the cigarette and tossed it into the ashes of the campfire.

He closed his eyes.

The sweet aroma of her hair was in his face. The soft and warm touch of her skin was . . .

Cord's eyes snapped open.

"You're a damn fool," he said aloud.

"There's no need of you sleeping on a cot," James said. "The bed is plenty big for both of us. Always has been."

"And if I roll over in my sleep and hit you in the ribs?" Sarah said. "A week in a cot won't kill me, James, but if I sleep a week in the bed, it might kill you."

James nodded. "Maybe you're right," he said. "I was asleep when Cord left. I didn't get to say a proper thank-you for what he done."

"Seth and I thanked him, James," Sarah said.

"He killed Parker's son and saved my life," James said. "A man should do the thanking himself. Did he say where he was headed?"

"I don't think he's headed anywhere, James," Sarah said. "At least that's the impression I got when he left."

"After killing the Parker boy, staying around here would be a damn fool thing to do," James said.

"Nonetheless, I think he will be staying close by," Sarah said. "He gave us a rifle and a forty-five pistol to protect ourselves with."

"Gave us?" James said. "Why would he give us a rifle and pistol?"

"For exactly the reasons you said," Sarah said. "Parker isn't done with this after his son was killed. We all know that. And you with those ribs, he thought the rifle and pistol might be necessary."

"It might be at that," James said. "What kind of rifle?"

"A Winchester rifle. And a Colt revolver."

"I've been meaning to get a Winchester," James said. "I will pay him for both the next time we meet."

"All right, James," Sarah said. "Mr. Coy left you some sleeping powder to mix with water. Do you want some for the pain?"

"That might be best," James said.

"I'll be right back," Sarah said.

Sarah went to the kitchen and opened one of the small packets of sleeping powder and dumped it into a glass, cranked the pump several times and filled the class with cold water. She stirred the water with a spoon and then carried it to James.

"Can you help me sit up so I can drink it?" James said.

Sarah set the glass on the small night table and then gently placed her arms under his back. Together they managed to get James into a sitting position without causing him too much pain.

"We are caught in the middle, James," Sarah said as she handed him the glass. "Parker will never buy us out now. We have no choice but to stay put."

"I know it," James said. "We'll outlast him."

"Outlast him?" Sarah said. "And what happens to Seth if the shooting starts?"

James sipped from the glass. "Tastes awful," he said. "I think it's time we involved the US marshal from Casper. Are you up to taking a ride to see Uggla in the morning? Ask him to come talk to me when he gets a chance."

"All right, James," Sarah said. "Finish drinking that and get some rest. I'll be right outside if you need me."

James finished the sleeping mixture and Sarah helped him recline. Then she kissed him lightly on the lips and blew out the lantern on the night table.


Parker held the deck. It was a matter of seeing what hand he dealt.

Best get your mind wrapped around what needed to be done, Cord thought.

Like on Sherman's March to the Sea, when the orders were

to kill anything that moved and burn anything that didn't.

Once you wrapped your mind around what needed to be done, doing it became easy.

# FORTY-SIX

"How was your trip, Mr. Parker?" Teasel said when he entered Parker's office at the ranch house.

"Fine," Parker said. "Close the door."

Teasel closed the door and walked to the desk. Parker was having coffee. A full pot rested on the serving tray on the desk.

"Have a cup and sit," Parker said.

"Thank you," Teasel said, filled a cup from the pot and took a seat.

"Have you thought about what I told you the other day?" Parker said.

"Yes, Mr. Parker."

"And what are your thoughts?"

"You can count on me, Mr. Parker," Teasel said.

"For anything?" Parker said.

Teasel nodded. "For anything."

"Pick a dozen men from the hands," Parker said. "Find the men who rode with John if they're still around. Tell them I'll pay each one of them one thousand dollars in gold to drive these farmers out of the territory. You will lead this bunch. Any questions?"

Teasel sipped coffee and then said, "No, sir."

"Mind your father until I return," Sarah said. "Make sure you stay by his side and get him what he needs. I should be back before noon or so."

Seth watched Sarah climb onto the buckboard.

"Yes, Ma," Seth said.

Sarah cracked the reins, and the team moved the wagon forward. Seth watched until Sarah drove the wagon onto the road and was out of sight before he turned and went into the house.

Sarah traveled about two miles along the road until she reached the fork. Left would take her to the Jones farm and beyond, right to the Uggla farm. She went to the right where the road followed the creek most of the way.

She paused, locked the brake, stepped down from the buckboard and waited for the sudden wave of nausea to pass. When her stomach settled, she climbed back onto the buckboard, released the brake and continued on.

Uggla's farm was about five miles to the west.

Sarah rode about two miles and slowed the team to a stop when she spotted a lean-to down by the creek about a hundred yards away.

Sarah stayed perfectly still as her eyes scanned the area around the lean-to, but if anyone was about he wasn't making his presence known.

There wasn't a horse tied or hobbled. Whoever was camping was out at the moment. She turned the team and slowly rode toward the campsite.

Sarah stopped the wagon twenty feet from the lean-to. She reached into her handbag for the Colt revolver given to her by Cord and cocked it.

"Hello?" she said.

Sarah's greeting was met with silence.

She climbed down from the buckboard and held the Colt revolver in two hands as she approached the lean-to. A coffeepot rested in the ashes of the fire. She reached down and

215

touched the pot. It was still warm to the touch.

She looked into the lean-to and there by the bedroll was a canvas sack she recognized as Cord's laundry bag.

Sarah turned and quickly scanned the area, the creek, the road.

"Cord!" Sarah shouted.

She felt her heart skip a beat and race inside her chest.

"Cord, where are you!" she shouted.

Wherever he was, it wasn't here. Sarah uncocked the Colt and held it by her side. Maybe if he was close by or returning to his camp, she could wait for him.

She could fire a shot. He would hear it and return to his camp.

"No," Sarah said aloud and returned to the wagon.

"Help me out of this bed, son," James said. "I can't take any more of this laying around like some sack of potatoes."

Seth approached the bed. "Ma said . . ."

"I can guess what your ma said," James said. "Now help me up. I would like to sit on the porch and get some fresh air and sun."

Sarah arrived at the Uggla farm shortly after ten in the morning. Amy, Uggla's fifteen-year-old daughter, was beating a rug slung over a clothesline.

"Mrs. Johansen?" Amy said.

Sarah parked the wagon and climbed down.

"James asked me to speak to your father," Sarah said.

"He's in the barn," Amy said.

Uggla walked out of the barn to Sarah. "I thought I heard your voice," he said. "How is James?"

"Mending," Sarah said. "He asked me to speak with you."

Cord rode back to his camp after scouting the Parker ranch and spotted wagon marks on the grass leading up to his lean-to.

He dismounted and walked down the road a bit with his horse in tow. The wagon came from the east and veered off the road to his lean-to and then turned back onto the road ten yards or so further down.

Cord walked his horse into his camp.

Nothing had been disturbed.

Cord knew from the direction the wagon came from that the road led directly to the Johansen farm. West on the road took you to the Uggla farm and beyond that the Jones place.

The impression left on the grass by the wagon wheels wasn't deep enough for it to be one of Parker's freight wagons. One rider—two riders at most—and an empty bed.

James Johansen couldn't have been fit enough to stand on his own yet, much less take a ride in a wagon.

Cord quickly broke camp and packed his gear away in his large canvas sack, hung it on the saddle and followed the wagon tracks on the road.

Cord was prone on a hill that overlooked the house and barn of the Uggla farm. His horse was tied to a thick tree out of sight. He had his army rifle scope and scanned the wagon.

It was Johansen's.

Cord kept the scope on the house. After a time Uggla, his wife and Sarah came out. They walked to the wagon where Sarah climbed onto the buckboard. A few parting words were said, and Sarah started on the return trip.

Cord let her get five hundred yards down the road, then he mounted up and followed her from the hills.

He kept his distance. Only after she was safely home and inside the house did he turn and ride away.

Earlier, when Sarah came by his camp, Cord had been scouting the Parker ranch. Although his ranch was vast, with tens of thousands of acres, it was nestled in a valley. The road leading to the Parker ranch was surrounded on both sides by rolling hills and short mountains.

He walked his horse up the tallest peak that overlooked the Parker home, about a thousand feet or so in elevation, and camped out for a bit.

He used the rifle scope to check things close up. Parker wasn't around, but his foreman Teasel was in front of the bunkhouse with a dozen men or so. They were having a meeting about something with Teasel in charge.

After fifteen minutes or so the meeting broke up, and the dozen men went to the corral to saddle their horses.

Teasel walked across the wide yard to the house, opened the door and went inside.

Cord watched the dozen cowboys ride out and head west. After a few minutes they were out of his sight. Cord rolled a cigarette, sat back to smoke it and kept watch on the house.

Parker and Teasel came out with cups of coffee, took seats on the porch and engaged in conversation.

Cord used the rifle scope to gauge the distance from his position to the porch. He estimated it to be one thousand yards, give or take a few, and not a very difficult shot at all with the Sharps rifle.

Cord returned to his horse and walked him down the mountain back to the road. Parker's war was coming.

There was no getting away from it.

And, like in 1863, he made the war his own.

# FORTY-SEVEN

"I'm not against the idea, James," Uggla said. "I'll go myself to Casper and speak to the marshal, but I'm not exactly sure what to tell him. I've been thinking about it on the ride over here, and as far as I can figure, Parker hasn't committed any federal crimes. His son busted up a vegetable patch and is dead for his trouble."

James, Sarah and Uggla were seated in chairs on the porch. Sarah served coffee and James lit up his pipe. If he were in any great pain, James hid it well, Uggla thought.

"I know that," James said. "All I'm asking is for the marshal to come down here to investigate our situation and talk to everybody involved. A stern warning from a federal officer might just back up Parker some and give us some breathing room."

"It's a day's ride to and back from Casper if you leave at sunup," Sarah said. "If you don't want to go, I'll make the trip myself."

"Now hold on," Uggla said. "I didn't say I wouldn't go. I just want to know exactly what I'm telling the marshal."

"Well, now you know," James said.

"No need to get angry, James," Uggla said. "I'll leave first thing in the morning."

"We'll leave first thing in the morning," Sarah said.

"There's no need of you . . . ," James said.

"I'm sure Mr. Uggla would agree that I can better convey the dire need we have for the marshal than he can," Sarah said.

219

"Mr. Uggla can act as my protector on the ride to and from Casper so there is no need for you to fret."

Uggla nodded at James. "She makes a good point, James," he said. "Most times I can't find the right word. She speaks so much better than me."

James looked at Sarah.

Sarah nodded.

James caved in, nodded and said, "I guess it does make sense at that."

"Mr. Uggla, can you pick me up at dawn?" Sarah said. "I'll pack a picnic lunch we can eat on the way."

Cord picked a new spot along the creek where he wouldn't be detected after dark. He made camp, built a fire and made a supper of beans, bacon and a few hard biscuits from the package he got in town. He washed it all down with cups of coffee.

After rinsing out the cookware in the creek, Cord spread his bedroll in the lean-to, rolled a cigarette and settled in beside the quickly diminishing campfire.

His mind was around it now, the killing that was to come. To stop Parker and beat him at his own game, he would have to stop Parker from implementing whatever plan he had devised.

That meant proactive killing.

Not self-defense, as with Parker's son, but outright murder, as with Sherman's March to the Sea.

His decision made, Cord knew pulling the trigger would be the easy part.

For once it was a fine night for sleeping. The heat wave broke and the house was filled with cool night air. James was mending quickly and no longer needed sleeping powders to get some rest. In a few days, Sarah should be able to pack up the cot and sleep in the bed.

Sarah went over in her mind what she would say to the US marshal in Casper come tomorrow. Parker was a well-known, well-respected and powerful man in Wyoming. It wouldn't be easy to convince the marshal to ride down to Brooks and investigate Parker's activities when Parker hadn't yet committed a crime.

To be honest with herself, it was a welcome relief to have her nightly thoughts filled with something besides Cord.

Slowly her mind shut down and her eyes closed and just before sleep took her a bitter odor fluttered into the room on the soft breeze.

Harsh.

Acrid.

Sarah opened her eyes and sat up on the cot.

Smoke.

Sarah didn't bother to grab her robe as she went outside and stood on the porch. The smell of smoke was thicker, more pungent, and the air was heavy with it. She went inside and gently shook James awake.

"Smoke," Sarah said. "Can you stand?"

James managed to get out of bed on his own and followed Sarah outside to the porch. He looked up at the bright moon where it illuminated the clouds surrounding it and could see the dark billowing smoke as it rose upward, caught in the breeze coming from the west.

"It doesn't smell like wood burning," Sarah said.

"That's because it ain't," James said.

"Then what?"

James lowered himself into a chair, feeling the tightness in his ribs.

Sarah sat in the seat beside him.

"James, what's burning?" Sarah said.

"Crops."

Mal Jones opened his eyes and knew immediately his field was burning. He didn't need to shake Keri, as she smelled it too and was instantly awake.

Wearing nightshirts and with bare feet, Mal and Keri raced outside to the porch. The light given off by their crops burning was intense, and so was the heat on the night breeze.

Their son, sleepy-eyed, came out behind them.

"What's happening?" Cal said.

"Stay here on the porch," Mal said.

"But, Pa . . . ," Cal said.

"Stay here," Mal snapped.

Mal and Keri raced off the porch and ran the entire way to their fields.

All of their crops were burning.

The heat was too intense to get close. The smoke was so thick and black, they had to cover their face with their night-shirts.

"Parker's men," Mal said.

Mal turned and ran back to the house with Keri right behind him. When they reached the house, Mal raced inside.

Keri stayed on the porch with Cal.

"Ma?" Cal said.

Keri hugged her son tightly.

Mal came back out holding his Winchester rifle and dressed ready to ride.

"Where are you going?" Keri said.

"To see Parker," Mal said.

"No you are not," Keri said and grabbed Mal's arm.

Mal broke free and walked down the porch steps to the corral.

Keri rushed down beside Mal.

"They'll kill you," Keri said.

"Then they'll kill me," Mal said as he opened the corral gate.

Mal reached for his saddle that hung over a fence railing.

Keri grabbed Mal by the shirt.

"Get off me, woman," Mal said. He shoved Keri backward.

"Mal, listen to me. Please," Keri said.

"I had enough listening," Mal said.

Keri grabbed Mal again. He shoved her harder, and she fell to the ground.

Cal came running into the corral.

"Ma, Ma!" Cal shouted.

"Take your ma inside," Mal said as he slung the saddle over his horse.

Cord saddled his horse and rubbed his neck.

"I know you're tired. I know you want to sleep," Cord whispered. "But I need you to run for me like you were racing in Kentucky."

Mal rode his horse from the corral to the road with Keri and Cal screaming at him to stop.

As he neared the road, Mal turned his horse. Just as he did so, Cord came racing in and blocked his path.

"Where you going, Mal?" Cord said.

"To see Parker," Mal said. "Do you see that fire, that smoke? Parker burned me out. Now I'm grateful to you for saving my life, but get out of my way."

"Stop him!" Keri yelled. "Mr. Cord, please stop him."

"Give me the road, Cord," Mal said and pointed the Winchester at him. "I'm serious."

"Sure," Cord said and moved his horse to the right.

As Mal rode past him, Cord flicked his left leg out and up

and kicked Mal in the jaw, knocking him to the ground.

In an instant, Cord was out of the saddle with his heavy .44 revolver in his hand. As Mal rose up, Cord knocked him out with a quick slap to the face.

"Is it Uggla's place?" Sarah said.

James shook his head. "That smoke isn't close enough."

"Mal Jones?"

James nodded.

"Oh, dear God."

"God's got nothing to do with this," James said. "This is all Parker's doing."

Keri wiped Mal's face with a wet cloth after Cord carried him to the porch.

Cord rode down to the fields while she tended to Mal. He was gone about fifteen minutes before he rode back and dismounted.

"How is he?" Cord said.

"Hurt. He'll have a gut buster of a headache come morning, but he's alive and I thank you for that," Keri said. "The crops?"

Cord shook his head.

"All of them?"

"Afraid so."

Cal came onto the porch with a fresh basin of water and set it beside Keri.

"Pa going to be all right?" Cal said.

"He'll be fine," Keri said. "You should thank Mr. Cord for saving his life."

"No need," Cord said. "It's too dark to follow any tracks. Okay if I stay in your barn tonight and get a fresh start in the morning?"

"No, you don't stay in the barn, Mr. Cord," Keri said. "You stay in our home."

## FORTY-EIGHT

Uggla rode his wagon onto the Johansen farm shortly before the dawn broke. Sarah and James sat on the porch illuminated by a lit lantern.

They were drinking coffee.

James was smoking his pipe.

"I made biscuits and jam and coffee," Sarah said. "Have some before we leave."

Uggla dismounted from his buckboard and climbed the steps. "They burned out Mal Jones last night," he said.

"We know," James said. "We could smell it clear over to here."

"Parker," Uggla said.

"At least we now have a legitimate complaint to file with the marshal," Sarah said.

"Except no one saw anybody do it," James said.

"It's still a reason to consider," Sarah said.

Sarah poured coffee for Uggla and held out the plate of biscuits.

"Thank you," Uggla said.

"Eat your fill," James said. "It's a long ride to Casper."


Cord had breakfast with Keri and Cal before sunup.

Fresh eggs, bacon, fried potatoes and coffee. The strong aroma of breakfast woke Mal. He stumbled from the bedroom with the suspenders on his pants hanging loose.

Mal looked at Cord.

"Are we running a hotel now?" Mal said.

"Mal, Mr. Cord saved your life last night, even if you're too thickheaded to know it," Keri said. "Now sit down, shut up and have some breakfast."

Amazingly, Mal sat and looked at Keri.

Cal looked at Cord, and Cord winked at the boy.

"Well, give a man some food, then," Mal said.

Cord saddled his horse and met Mal and Keri at the porch.

"That Winchester rifle you have, keep it close," Cord said. "I doubt they'll be back to your place, but keep it handy anyway."

"You can bet I will," Mal said.

"If I pick up their tracks, I'll stop by and let you know," Cord said.

Keri handed Cord a sack.

"Biscuits and corn dodgers for the ride," Keri said.

"Thank you," Cord said and mounted his horse.

It wasn't very difficult at all to pick up the tracks of a dozen horses in the soft dirt and rocks beside the burned-out field. In the aftermath of the fire that had destroyed Mal's crops Cord smelled the lingering odor of kerosene lantern oil.

He saw it in his mind. The dozen riders with jugs of lantern oil rode onto the fields, tossed the oil everywhere, lit torches and flung them to start the fire.

After they'd burned the crops, they rode west and to the north in the general direction of the Parker ranch.

Tracking them on dirt was easy, but when they reached open plains, Cord had to dismount and search for signs in the soft grass.

It wasn't much different from tracking Rebels during the war. One or two on horseback left few traces as they rode through, but a dozen horses running flat out kicked up divots of dirt and grass. Those he could spot ten yards away.

Cord rubbed his horse's neck as he removed a carrot stick from his saddlebag. Cord took a bite and then gave the rest to the horse.

"We'll walk a while," Cord said. "How would that be?"

Walking his horse served two purposes. The first was it saved the horse's strength for times when he really needed it, such as tracking out in the open and there was a chance of ambush.

The second was that a horse unmounted made a softer impression in the earth than a horse with two hundred pounds in the saddle. If someone was tracking him, it would be harder to pick up the tracks.

After a mile or so on foot, Cord reached the road that he knew would lead him directly to the pass between the hills and the Parker ranch.

He mounted up and followed the dozens of tracks for several miles to the turnoff that went to only one place, right to Parker's doorstep.

Cord went straight and followed the road for a half mile and then dismounted in front of the tall hill that overlooked the Parker ranch.

Cord stroked his horse's neck. "I know it's a long way up and we just did this, but if I leave you here, someone might come along," he said.

The trek to the top took thirty minutes, as Cord took it slow and easy. The last thing he needed was for his horse to slip on loose rock and break a leg. He would have to put him down using the bayonet so as not to fire a shot and alert Parker and every hand on his ranch. Even so, inside of a day, the swarming buzzards would alert them below that something large was dead in the hills. They would investigate and know they were being watched.

Cord had spent years training his horse and the big male was sure-footed and unafraid of rocks or heights, and they arrived at the top unscathed.

Cord rewarded his horse with several large sugar cubes from the saddlebags. Then he sat with the binoculars and rolled a cigarette.

With the binoculars Cord scanned the grounds. The large corral where the hands penned their horses overnight held fourteen animals. He figured Parker kept forty hands. All but fourteen were out working.

It was a safe bet the fourteen horses belonged to the men who burned out Mal Jones the night before and they were sleeping late. Parker probably had another target for them, but there was no telling which farm was in his sights.

If Parker was around, he was in the house and out of sight.

Cord set the binoculars aside and removed Keri's sack and his canteen from the saddle. He munched on a few biscuits and corn dodgers and sipped water. Then he rolled another smoke and waited.

Between ten and ten thirty by the placement of the sun, cowhands started filing out of the bunkhouse and walked to the chow hall, a large building to the left of the bunkhouse.

Cord used the binoculars to study their faces so he would recognize them later if need be and the situation demanded it.

He didn't see Teasel in the group.

The ranch foreman had to know about last night's raid on the Jones farm.

Either took part in it or knew about it.

Teasel didn't strike Cord as the kind of man who would take part in burning people out of their farms and homes, but who really ever knew about a person until that person revealed all to you?

The hands were all inside the chow hall.

Cord packed the binoculars away and walked his horse slowly back down the hill.

★ ★ ★ ★ ★

As they entered the town line for Casper, it occurred to Sarah that this was her first visit to the city. A welcoming sign on Main Street claimed a population of just over one thousand people.

It seemed to her that every one of those thousand people was on the streets.

"I see the town sheriff's office over there," Uggla said. "He should know where the marshal's office is located."

Uggla drove the wagon to the sheriff's office and parked the wagon.

"I won't be but a minute," Uggla said.

While Uggla was gone, Sarah observed the streets. Cowboys on horseback, wagons full of freight, women in colorful summer dresses and hats, everybody seemed to be in one big hurry.

Uggla was gone not more than five minutes.

"The courthouse at the edge of town," he said.

Uggla drove the wagon to the edge of town where the red-brick, two-story courthouse sat alone. A bed of flowers adorned the neatly trimmed front lawn. The flag hung high on a pole and waved softly in the slight breeze.

Uggla and Sarah climbed the twenty stone steps to the courthouse doors and entered the large, polished lobby.

A man behind a desk looked at them. "Can I help you?" he said.

"We'd like to see the marshal?" Uggla said. "Is he in?"

"Sign the log," the man said.

On the desk were an open logbook, pen and inkwell.

Uggla and Sarah took turns signing the book.

The man said, "Follow the hall past the courtroom and offices to the last door on the right. The marshal is in."

"Thank you," Uggla said.

Uggla and Sarah followed the hall past the courtroom, offices for prosecutor and defense, court clerk and administration to the office of US Marshal Franklin Harper.

Uggla opened the door and he and Sarah entered the office.

Cord reached the Jones farm shortly after one in the afternoon.

Mal met him at the corral.

"Put your horse in the corral," Mal said. "Feed and water him and we'll talk in the house."

"I remember you from the Pettibone trial," Harper said to Sarah. "And I understand your concern regarding Mr. Parker."

"Concern?" Sarah said. "Did you understand when I told you Parker's men burned an entire field of crops last night?"

"Mrs. Johansen, I am a US marshal, and I represent the law," Harper said. "Unless you can produce a witness who saw Mr. Parker or his men burn the field and can prove it, I am powerless to do anything about it. Can you produce a witness?"

"No," Sarah said. "But you are aware of the tensions that exist between Mr. Parker and the farmers?"

"I am, but tension isn't a crime, especially on a federal level."

"So you're going to do nothing?" Sarah said.

"I didn't say that," Harper said. "I have to testify in court in Medicine Bow on a federal matter. Once I'm finished there, I'll ride up and do some checking on things, speak to Mr. Parker and some of the farmers."

"When will that be?" Sarah said.

"Ten days. That is the best I can do," Harper said.

"I'll hold you to what you just said," Sarah said. "Good day, Marshal."

Keri served Cord hot biscuits and coffee at the kitchen table, and then she sent Cal outside to do chores while Cord filled them in on his morning.

"I didn't need to track them to know who was behind it," Mal said.

Cord bit into a biscuit and washed it down with coffee. "This is just the beginning," Cord said.

"Any Parker man sets foot on my property gets shot," Mal said.

"They're done with you," Cord said. "They will pick a new target and keep burning crops until every farmer moves his family out or faces starvation."

"Then we'll get together and fight," Mal said.

"And then all of you will leave widows and children without fathers," Cord said.

"We're not gunmen, but we are still men. You can't expect us to run like cowards," Mal said.

"Mr. Jones, just stay put here a while," Cord said. He looked at Keri. "You see to it that he doesn't leave the farm for any reason until this is over."

Mal looked carefully at Cord.

"Parker isn't going to like you changing sides," Mal said.

"Me and Parker ain't related anymore," Cord said. "Besides, whoever said I was on his side?"

"Seth and I made supper," James said to Uggla when he and Sarah returned at dusk. "Why not join us and tell us all about the meeting."

Uggla nodded. "My missus isn't expecting me back for supper," he said. "So I might as well."

Cord was finishing a plate of beans and bacon with some of Keri Jones's biscuits at his campsite by the creek.

Dusk was settling in and brought the promise of a cool, clear night with it.

After rinsing off the cookware in the creek, Cord rolled a

cigarette and sat back against a tree to mull things over in his mind.

Another burning was sure to follow. Parker wasn't going to quit after one. He wanted them all out, and after his offer to buy failed and his son was killed, Parker's frame of mind was definitely set on revenge.

The Jones farm wasn't the closest to Parker's ranch. The Uggla place was, but Cord was certain in his mind Jones was chosen first because of his color.

The one to target, in Cord's mind, was James Johansen. He was the obvious leader in the group. If he fell and pulled out, the others would surely follow.

There was no way to know for certain Parker's mind, but it . . .

Smoke.

Cord stood up and scanned the sky. Dusk, it was still light enough to see clouds and the quickly rising smoke and he knew another field was burning.

It was far. Past the Jones place.

It had to be Uggla's.


Uggla, James and Sarah stood on the Johansen porch and watched the thick smoke rise up to meet the darkening sky.

"That's my place," Uggla said.

"You don't know for sure," James said.

"I know which way the wind blows over my fields," Uggla said.

Uggla ran down the steps to his wagon.

"Hold on, I'm going with you," James said.

Uggla climbed onto the buckboard. "Appreciate that, James, but you're in no shape for the kind of riding I gotta do."

With a crack of the reins, Uggla raced his team onto the road.

Uggla ran his team as hard as they could go and made it to the fork in the road in less than thirty minutes. He took the turn for his farm, cracked the reins and his team responded with more speed.

After a mile or so, the hitch started to crack under the strain of the massive horses pulling the wagon with so much force.

"Ayah . . . ayah . . . move it, you nags!" Uggla yelled and snapped the reins again.

The two massive quarter horses yanked the wagon forward. The hitch split in two and, freed of its restraint, the wagon went sailing out of control and off the road. Uggla was unable to steer or stop the speeding wagon, and it struck a tall tree head-on. Uggla went up and over and smashed into the tree headfirst.

"Oh, dear God," Sarah said as she watched the black smoke pass in front of clouds lit by the nearly full moon.

"There is nothing we can do about it tonight," James said.

"And when they come for us tomorrow or the next night?"

"By God, busted ribs or not, I will fight them," James said.

"And if you do, they won't break your ribs. They will shoot you like a rabid dog," Sarah said.

"Well, what would you have me do?" James said. "Run? Hide? Show my only son that his father is a coward?"

Sarah stared at James.

"I was waiting for the right time to tell you this, James," Sarah said. "But Seth will not be your only son. I'm pregnant. I'm sure of it, and I'm sure it will be a boy."

James softened and smiled at Sarah. "Are you sure? When did you find out?"

"For the past few mornings, I have had the morning sickness," Sarah said. "I'm sure. I'm also sure that if you challenge Parker's men, my next child will be born without a father."

"Well, what am I supposed to do? Sit back and watch them

burn us out?" James said. "You said that marshal won't be here for . . ."

"I know what I said," Sarah said. "But Seth and the new child will need a father to provide for them. You can't do that from the grave."

James nodded. "All right," he said softly.

Sarah looked at the smoke against the clouds.

James placed his arm around her.

"We've been blessed," James said.

Looking at the smoke, Sarah nodded.

"Yes," she said.

# FORTY-NINE

Cord rode to the road just after sunrise and turned right. The fork in the road was about a mile to the east. He planned to take the road at the fork to the Uggla farm. He rode about a half mile and stopped when he spotted a hitched team without a wagon in an empty field of tall grass.

Cord dismounted and walked his horse to the team in case they spooked at a stranger. They didn't. As he approached the team, Cord dug out sugar cubes and gave a few to each massive horse.

Cord rubbed their necks as they munched the cubes.

"Where's your wagon?" Cord said. "Where's your owner?"

Cord looked down the road. Then he mounted up and rode back to the road to look for the wagon.

He rode about three quarters of a mile and found it.

Smashed up against the base of a tall tree.

The rider was on the grass beside the wagon, facedown.

Cord dismounted and turned the rider over. His face was pretty smashed up, but Cord recognized him as Uggla, one of the farmers, and most likely the one whose farm was burned out last night.

In the morning, Katherine and Amy Uggla were inspecting the damage to the fields. The destruction was total. Every acre was charred and acrid-smelling, without a stalk of corn or strand of wheat left unscathed.

"Oh, Ma," Amy said. "When Pa sees this . . ."

Katherine heard a rider arrive at the house.

"Quiet," Katherine said.

After a few seconds, Amy said, "Maybe it's Pa?"

"No wagon," Katherine said.

From her apron pocket, Katherine withdrew Uggla's Colt revolver.

"Ma!" Amy said.

"Be quiet. When we see who it is, if I tell you to hide, that is what you will do," Katherine said.

Katherine and Amy slowly walked the acre back to their house. When Cord, the team and a body slung over the back of one of the horses were in view, the revolver fell from Katherine's hand and she ran to the house screaming.

Amy followed her mother.

"Dear God, no!" Katherine screamed when she reached her dead husband.

"I thank you for bringing my husband home," Katherine said.

Shirtless, Cord set the shovel against the side of the porch.

"It's done," Cord said. "He's buried beside that tree in back of the house. Where is your daughter?"

"In the house," Katherine said. "I'm afraid she is taking this very hard."

Cord slipped on his shirt.

"I made tea," Katherine said. "I don't know why, but in times of stress I always make tea. Will you have some with me?"

Cord nodded. He went up and sat beside Katherine. She had a tray set up with teapot, cups, milk and sugar. She poured tea, added sugar and a dash of milk and handed the cup to Cord.

He took a sip. "It's very good."

Katherine nodded. "My husband, he hated tea."

"Mrs. Uggla, stay in the house for the next few days," Cord

said. "They are through with you, but they will be out tonight after another farm. I will tell the others of your loss. I'm sure they will want to conduct a service."

Katherine sipped tea and nodded.

Cord finished his tea and stood up.

"Do you have any weapons?" he said.

"My husband's Colt revolver and Winchester rifle."

"Do you know how to use them?"

"Yes."

Cord nodded and stepped down off the porch, paused and turned around.

"What was your husband's name?" Cord said.

"Daniel."

"A fine name," Cord said.

Keri Jones started to cry when Cord stopped by the Jones farm to tell them the news.

"He was a good man," Mal said. "He and Johansen were the first to welcome us here. Our color never mattered a bit to him. He will be missed."

"Might you be able to inform some of the others?" Cord said.

"I'll ride over to Johansen this afternoon," Mal said.

"Can I impose on you for a bit of supplies?" Cord said. "Some beans, bacon and a bit of coffee."

"I'll get them," Keri said and went into the house.

Teasel entered the house and found Parker at his desk in the den. Parker was working on the books using pen and ink.

"You sent for me, Mr. Parker?" Teasel said.

"Yes," Parker said. "Have a seat. The coffee is fresh."

Teasel reached for a cup, filled it from the pot on the table beside the desk and took a seat.

"I think we've softened them up enough to go for the knockout blow," Parker said. "Tonight hit the Johansen place. Burn all their crops, then the barn and everything in it. Don't hurt them, though. Johansen is the leader of these sodbusters. Once he's ruined, I'll be able to get every one of them to sell at my price."

Teasel sipped from his cup and nodded.

"Is the gunfighter still hanging around?" Parker said.

"I haven't seen him, but he's still around," Teasel said.

"Good," Parker said. "I have a surprise for him in town. I'll be at the hotel for a few days. Report to me there."

James, Sarah and Seth were just sitting down to supper when they heard a wagon arrive outside the open kitchen window.

James went to see who it was.

"Why, that's Mal Jones," James said.

James, Sarah and Seth went out to the porch to greet him.

"Mal, kind of late to be riding around, isn't it?" James said.

"Uggla is dead," Mal said.

Cord broke his camp two hours before sunset. He was on the far side of the tall hill. He hobbled his horse in a thicket of trees well off the road, then climbed the hill with plenty of time to spare.

He brought the binoculars with him.

The ranch, house and bunkhouse were quiet, still. He counted fourteen horses in the corral. The majority of the hands had yet to return or they were sleeping on the range.

Then, one by one, a dozen hands filed out of the bunkhouse and walked to the corral. They each held a Winchester rifle and an unlit torch. They saddled their horses in the corral, put rifle and torch in the long rifle sleeve and waited.

For Teasel to exit the house and join them.

As they rode out, Cord checked the placement of the sun. About an hour to dusk.

They had a long way to ride and wanted an early start.

Cord walked down the hill to his horse, removed the leather strip from his front legs and mounted up.

Cord stayed hidden in the thicket until he saw the bunch ride by, led by Teasel.

"Well, we best turn in early if we're going to ride out to pay our respects in the morning," James said.

"Are you up to such a long ride?" Sarah said.

"I'm not ready to get behind a plow, but I can ride in a wagon," James said.

"Ma, I don't understand any of this," Seth said.

"I know," Sarah said. "Go inside and wash your hands and face. Use the baking soda to brush your teeth. Then get to bed."

Seth kissed Sarah on the cheek.

"Night, Ma. Night, Pa," Seth said and went inside.

Sarah and James sat in their chairs on the porch and watched dusk turn to night and the stars come out.

"We best go in, too," James said.

After an hour's ride, Cord knew the cowboys' destination was the Johansen farm.

Even on a dark road, the group wasn't hard to track. Thirteen horses riding at a steady pack made a noise you could hear for a hundred yards or more at night.

They made it easier to track when Cord spotted bright dots of light ahead, and he knew they'd lit the torches.

Cord broke off the road to the left and used the light of the moon to travel to the backside of the Johansen farm. He rode hard and arrived at the base of a steep hill that overlooked the

Johansen fields.

He tied off his horse, took the Sharps rifle and a box of ammunition and climbed the hill to the top.

Two hundred yards below, the fields were dimly lit in moonlight. He judged the distance at four hundred yards.

Suddenly he was thirsty and wished he thought to bring the canteen.

No matter.

There was time for a smoke so he rolled a cigarette, lit up and enjoyed the short quiet before the storm.

# FIFTY

Cord spotted the lit torches and estimated the Parker hirelings were ten minutes or so from arriving at the Johansen fields.

He removed the long scope from his belt, placed it into the grooves on the Sharps rifle and locked it into place with a twist.

Cord watched the torches grow larger, brighter.

"Come on, you bastards, if you're coming," he said aloud.

Led by Teasel, the dozen riders arrived at the fields. They wore white spook hats with the eyes and mouth cut away. Cord knew Teasel by his horse.

"Spread out, empty your bottles of kerosene and toss the torches just like before," Teasel ordered.

Cord took aim through the scope and shot the first rider to Teasel's left. Even before the rider hit the ground, Cord shot two more.

Teasel and the remaining nine riders froze in their saddles.

"You can't see me, Teasel. Even if you could, your Winchesters would never make a shot at the distance I am at!" Cord shouted. "You're in the moon's light and those torches are like beacons. Move, and I'll drill every last one of you."

"Who the hell is . . . ?" a rider said.

"Cord, and he can kill every one of us if he has a mind to," Teasel said.

"They'll be no burning tonight!" Cord shouted. "Go back to the ranch and tell Parker to get ready for me! Daniel Uggla is dead, and you're responsible! You and Parker! You tell him I'm

242

coming, and I'm bringing the archangel of death with me! You hear me, Teasel?"

"Bullshit," the rider to Teasel's right said and reached for his Winchester.

Cord killed him with one shot to the heart.

"I hear you, Cord!" Teasel shouted. "And we're going."

"Then go and expect to see me soon!" Cord shouted.

"What about our dead?" Teasel shouted.

"Take them with you! Two men dismount and load the dead on their horses. Then ride out single file and keep the torches lit!"

Two men dismounted and lifted the four dead men onto their horses.

"Don't double back or look for me!" Cord shouted. "You won't see me, but I'll see you, and if I see you I'll kill you on the spot! All of you!"

"This isn't over, gunfighter!" a rider shouted.

"Not by a long shot!" Cord shouted. "Move out!"

And just as Teasel turned his horse toward the path, James Johansen limped into the moonlight with the Winchester rifle Cord gave Sarah.

Directly behind James, Sarah held onto her husband's shirt.

"You men come to burn our fields!" James shouted. "I'll kill every one of you bastards where you sit."

"James, stop it," Sarah said. "Give me that rifle before . . ."

Ignoring James, Teasel cracked his reins and rode off into the dark, quickly followed by his men.

James and Sarah watched the men file off their fields until none were left.

"I don't understand," James said. "Who did the shooting?"

Sarah scanned the dark hills overlooking the fields.

"Mr. Cord!" she shouted. "I know you're up there!"

"The gunfighter?" James said and winced in pain.

"James?" Sarah said.

"I'm all right," James said.

A moment later the rifle fell from his grasp and James grabbed his ribs. Sarah held James by his right arm and he leaned his weight onto her.

"Mr. Cord, we could do with the use of your horse!" Sarah shouted.

"No need of that," James said.

"It is three acres back to the house, and you're in a cold sweat as it is," Sarah said.

"I don't hear anything," James said. "Maybe he left already."

A moment later Cord, framed by the moon, rode over the hill to the bottom and dismounted beside Sarah and James.

"His ribs," Sarah said. "Help him onto the saddle."

"I can manage," James said. He reached for the saddle horn and placed his left foot in the stirrup and nearly passed out from the pain in his side.

"Here," Cord said. He placed his hands under James's foot and gently lifted him into the saddle.

"Obliged," James said.

Cord held the reins and started walking back to the house.

Sarah clasped her hands behind her back so Cord wouldn't see them shaking and fell into step with him.

"Mal Jones told us you found Mr. Uggla's body," Sarah said.

Cord turned his head slightly and looked at her. In the pale moonlight her skin appeared the color of milk, flawless and beautiful.

"His team broke free of his wagon and he crashed into a tree," Cord said. "He must have died on impact."

"And tonight?" Sarah said.

"I scouted out Parker's ranch," Cord said. "I followed his men here and stopped them before they burned out your crops."

"How many did you kill?"

"Four."

"Dear God."

Cord grinned. "I don't know much, but I know God's got nothing to do with this," he said.

"How can you joke after killing four men?"

"Would you rather I let them burn you out?"

"No."

The house came into view. Seth was on the porch with the lantern lit.

"Pa!" Seth shouted as he ran down the steps.

"He's all right," Cord said as he turned to James. "Just passed out in the saddle."

"Seth, fill a basin with water and get some clean wraps for your father," Sarah said.

Seth ran into the house.

Cord gently removed James from the saddle, cradled him in his arms and carried him into the house.

Cord and Seth drank glasses of milk and ate apple pie at the kitchen table while Sarah tended to James in the bedroom.

She came into the kitchen holding the basin and dumped the water into the sink. She turned and looked at Cord.

"We are grateful to you, Mr. Cord," she said.

The urge to run and take him in her arms was almost overwhelming, but she choked it down and remained cordial.

Cord nodded, ate the last bit of apple pie on his plate and stood up. "I best be going now," he said.

"Can't you stay, Mr. Cord?" Seth said. "What if those men come back tonight?"

"They won't be back," Cord said.

"I think it's going to rain," Seth said. "You can't ride in the rain. Tell him, Ma. Tell him he should stay in the barn tonight."

Sarah stared at Cord.

"I'm sure Mr. Cord has someplace to go, Seth," she said.

"I'll see you again, son," Cord said and patted Seth's hair.

"I'll walk you out," Sarah said. "Seth, get back into bed."

"Aw, Ma," Seth said.

"Now."

Sarah followed Cord out to the porch.

Cord walked down the steps to his horse. Sarah wanted to follow him, but she did not. Cord looked up at her, and their eyes met and locked. An entire conversation took place without a word spoken.

Sarah ended the conversation by lowering her eyes.

Cord mounted his horse.

"Wait. Where are you going?" Sarah said.

"To finish this."

Sarah stayed on the porch and watched Cord ride off into the darkness. Then she went into the barn, sat on Seth's milking stool and had herself a good cry.

# FIFTY-ONE

Parker stood in front of Tobey's general store and waited for the Overland Stage to arrive. The afternoon sun was hot, and he was soaked through his shirt and suit jacket. A cold bottle of beer would have hit the spot, but he wouldn't be seen drinking on the street, so he settled for a bottle of Tobey's sarsaparilla.

Parker finished the bottle of soda pop, set it on the wood sidewalk and lit a cigar. The stage was late as usual. So late that the almost-foot-long cigar was down to just a few inches before he heard the thundering of the six horses as the stage arrived in town, turned a corner and stopped in front of Tobey's general store.

Two things of interest got off the stage.

The first was the mail sack carried by the driver.

The second was a tall, lean man named Jack Shea.

Predawn, Cord scanned the house, bunkhouse and mess hall of the Parker ranch from the hill about a thousand yards away.

As the sun rose, Cord saw the corral was filled with horses.

Smoke billowed up from the chimney in the mess hall as the two cooks got breakfast ready for the hands. Just after sunrise, one of the cooks came out and rang the bell hanging from the edge of the roof.

Moments later, sleepy, hungry cowhands filed out of the bunkhouse.

Cord took aim through the scope on the Sharps rifle and

shot a hand in the upper right thigh. Before he fell screaming, thirty hands hit the dirt and crawled for cover.

Cord fired two more times at the bell and rang it twice. Its loud chime echoed off the hills and took several seconds to fade away.

"Parker, you evil son of a bitch, show yourself!" Cord shouted. "You're responsible for Dan Uggla's death, and you have to answer for that! Do you hear me, Parker?"

Cord's answer was silence.

"Parker, show yourself, you coward!" Cord screamed.

The front door of the house opened and Teasel stepped out to the porch.

Teasel cupped his hands to his mouth. "Parker ain't here, Cord!" he shouted. "He's in town. Say what you came to say to me, and I'll see he gets your message."

"I could kill a third of you where you stand before you reach cover!" Cord said.

"I know that!" Teasel shouted. "What's your message?"

"Tell Parker his fight with the farmers is over!" Cord shouted. "It ends here and now, or I will hunt down and kill every one of his hands and then his cattle and finally him. I will burn this ranch like you burned those crops! You tell him that!"

"I'll need to ride to town!" Teasel shouted.

"You do that!" Cord shouted. "You men down there on your bellies, remember what I said."

A young-looking hand stood up. "You said Mr. Uggla is dead!" he shouted.

"Killed trying to save his crops that you burned!" Cord shouted.

"I don't know nothing about burning crops!" the young hand shouted. "Is Mrs. Uggla and Amy all right?"

"Mrs. Uggla lost her husband, the girl lost her father. How do you think they are?" Cord shouted.

"I didn't know," the hand shouted. "I have to see Amy! Don't shoot me! She's my . . . sweetheart."

"Get your horse and go!" Teasel shouted. "You're finished here."

"That suits me!" the hand shouted. He looked up at the hill. "You ain't gonna shoot me, right?"

"What's your name, boy?" Cord shouted.

"Jason!"

"I ain't gonna shoot you, Jason!" Cord shouted. "Get your horse and go."

Jason walked to the corral, grabbed his saddle off the fence railing and saddled his horse.

"Teasel, you best get to town and see Parker!" Cord shouted.

Then Cord turned and raced down the slope of the hill to the thicket where his hobbled horse was quietly eating tall sweet grass.

Parker served Jack Shea coffee before taking his seat behind his desk.

"Let's cut through it, Mr. Shea," Parker said. "You're here because you're a hired gun, and I need two people dead."

Shea sipped coffee and said, "I'm here because you agreed to my established fee."

"One thousand dollars per job is your standard fee," Parker said. "I will pay you five thousand, plus a thousand-dollar bonus upon completion."

"You must want them killed pretty bad for that kind of money," Shea said.

"The man I want dead the most is a gunfighter named Cord," Parker said. "Do you know him?"

"Of him," Shea said. "I hear he's pretty good."

"He murdered my son, so I want you to murder him," Parker said. "The other man is a farmer named Johansen. He's the leader of a group of farmers. With him out of the way, the others should pack up and leave without much trouble."

"Cord's a professional," Shea said. "It won't be too difficult to draw him into a fight, but what's going to provoke a farmer to pick up a gun and draw down on me?"

"Johansen is stubborn and prideful," Parker said. "He considers himself a reasonable man. I'll invite him to town to talk and leave the rest up to you."

"He got a family?"

"Wife, and a boy of about eight."

"I don't like witnesses, and boys of eight grow up to be men," Shea said.

"After Johansen is dead, you do what you think is best."

Shea sipped coffee and nodded. "I always do what I think is best," he said.

"We have a lot in common," Parker said.

The office door suddenly burst open and Teasel rushed in. "Mr. Parker, I'm sorry to interrupt but . . ."

"This is a private meeting, Mr. Teasel," Parker said.

"I understand that, sir, but this is an emergency," Teasel said.

---

"Step off that horse and I will shoot you dead," Katherine Uggla said to Jason when he arrived at the Uggla farm.

"Ma!" Amy said from the porch.

"Stay on the porch, Amy," Katherine said and kept the Winchester aimed at Jason.

"Mrs. Uggla, I didn't know what Mr. Parker was up to," Jason said. "I swear it. I just quit his outfit to tell you that and could have been killed doing so."

"How so?" Katherine said.

"That gunfighter Cord is up in the hills and made his intentions very clear with his long rifle," Jason said. "I think he's killed a bunch of Parker's men last night."

Katherine lowered the Winchester.

"I'm here to help, I swear on my mother," Jason said.

"Get down," Katherine said. "We'll talk."

"He has to be camped close by to keep an eye on my ranch," Parker said. "And he has to sleep sometime, doesn't he? Take a dozen men and track him on foot. When he's asleep you capture him, but don't kill him. Bring him back to the ranch alive. Understand?"

"I think I know where he might be camped," Teasel said.

"Then find him and bring him in," Parker said. "Mr. Shea will take care of the rest."

Teasel looked at Shea. "Shea? Jack Shea?" he said. "The gunfighter?"

"Feel better now?" Parker said.

"Some," Teasel said.

"Mr. Shea will be my guest at the hotel," Parker said. "I'll be there as well. Send a rider when Cord is in custody."

After a cold supper of biscuits, jerked beef and water, Cord pitched his lean-to by the creek and waited for dark to turn in early. He didn't want to risk a fire so close to the Parker ranch. He wanted to be up and in the saddle an hour before dawn to be on top of the hill for sunup.

He rolled a cigarette and smoked it before settling into his bedroll.

Earlier, after leaving the hill, he thought about visiting the Johansens' to see Sarah, but decided to check on Katherine and Amy Uggla instead.

He found Jason having lemonade on the porch with the two women.

At first Jason was afraid for his life. He owned a six-gun of course, but like most cowboys, he never had a reason to use it before. He knew what Cord was capable of having seen his ability earlier today.

"Relax, son. I'm not here to harm you," Cord said as he dismounted.

"I had nothing to do with Parker's doings," Jason said.

"I know," Cord said. "That six-shooter on your belt, can you use it?"

"If I have time enough to aim careful, I can usually hit what I aim at," Jason said.

"Maybe you might want to stay close by, just in case," Cord suggested.

"I plan to," Jason said.

"You too, Mrs. Uggla. Keep that Winchester handy," Cord advised.

Satisfied the Uggla women would be all right for now, he rode down to the creek near the Parker ranch and made camp.

Cord put the cigarette out and settled into his bedroll and waited for sleep.

Slowly his eyes closed. When they opened again, he was looking down the barrel of a cocked six-gun.

# FIFTY-TWO

Teasel gathered twelve hands eager for some payback and a fifty-dollar bonus and formed a posse.

Teasel knew from prior meetings with Cord that the gunfighter liked to camp near fresh water. Teasel also figured that Cord would camp relatively close to Parker's ranch to keep a close watch on things.

Teasel led the group on horseback shortly after dark. They rode about three miles and then hobbled the horses and set out on foot in two-man teams to search for Cord's lean-to camp.

Teasel went with a two-man team, each team covering different ground along the creek. The half-moon provided just enough light to be able to navigate without torches.

The search took four hours, but at around eleven in the evening, Teasel's team spotted a lean-to pitched close to the creek embankment.

A hundred feet from the lean-to, Teasel stopped the team and whispered, "Boots off. We don't want any noise as we make our approach."

Teasel and the two hands drew and cocked their six-shooters before tiptoeing to the lean-to, so the noise of cocking them didn't wake Cord.

The gunfighter was sound asleep in bedroll.

Teasel nodded, and a hand stuck his cocked revolver against Cord's cheek.

Instantly, Cord was awake.

"Don't move. Don't breathe. Don't twitch," Teasel said. "There are three of us and our guns are cocked. We'll get you before you clear leather."

Cord looked at Teasel.

"Stand up slow so my man can take your guns," Teasel said.

Cord, with the cocked revolver pressed against his face, slowly rose to his feet.

"Tall, ain't he?" the hand with his revolver in Cord's face said.

"Take his guns," Teasel said. "And then put your boots on."

The hands removed Cord's .44 Colt from its holster and the .38 from the shoulder rig and tucked them into their belts. One at a time they put on their boots.

"I apologize for this, but you are too dangerous a man for us not to take precautions," Teasel said and smacked Cord in the face with his heavy revolver.

Cord fell to his knees dripping blood from the nose and mouth.

"Put the boots to him," Teasel said.

The two hands started kicking Cord in the ribs, stomach and face until Cord fell over, nearly unconscious.

"Get some rope from his saddlebags and tie his hands," Teasel said. "Saddle his horse and throw him over. We'll walk him back to our horses."

When Cord opened his eyes, his legs were in shackles and his hands were tied with thick rope. He was in a dark, damp room that smelled of dirt and potatoes. A crack of light came in under a door frame.

He was in a root cellar. His guess was it was located at the Parker ranch.

He felt dried blood on his face, in his nose and mouth.

It was morning, but he had no idea what time it was or how

long he'd been unconscious.

There was a noise outside the door. It opened, light flooded into the cellar and Cord snapped his eyes shut.

The door closed halfway, and Cord opened his eyes and looked at the plump, middle-aged man holding a basin of water.

"I am Juan, Mr. Parker's cook," he said. "Mr. Teasel, he say to clean you up."

"Are you a Mex?" Cord said.

"I am, but I was born in Texas," Juan said.

"Where is Teasel?" Cord said.

"He go to town," Juan said. "Now hold still so I can fix your cuts."

Parker was having a steak in the hotel dining room when Teasel entered and took a seat at the table.

"Caught him asleep in his bedroll late last night," Teasel said. "I got him chained up in the root cellar."

Parker set down his knife and fork and stared at Teasel. Slowly, Parker's lips formed a smile.

"Is he hurt?"

"A mite busted up, but he's okay."

"Keep him there for now," Parker said. "After dark ride out to Johansen's. Tell him to meet me in the saloon around midnight tonight. Tell him I want to settle things like gentlemen and talk out our differences. Tell him I'll be alone, and the saloon will be closed except for the bartender."

"What if he won't come?" Teasel said.

"He'll come," Parker said. "He prides himself on being reasonable."

"Where is Shea?" Teasel said.

"Over having a drink at the saloon, I believe," Parker said. "I'd stay away from him if I was you. The man is a mite testy."

★  ★  ★  ★  ★

Teasel had no intention of seeking out or speaking to Shea. The meeting was strictly an accident.

As Teasel left the hotel, Shea was on his way in.

"Parker in there?" Shea said.

"Having a steak," Teasel said.

"You leaving?"

"Mr. Parker has asked me to invite Johansen to have a private talk with him tonight at the saloon," Teasel said.

Shea stared at Teasel for a long moment.

"I understand Johansen has a real pretty wife," Shea said. "I might look her up after—her and the boy—and express my condolences."

Teasel raised an eyebrow, but before he could say another word Shea walked past him and entered the saloon.

"I do not think they will get infected with all the alcohol I rubbed on them," Juan said when he finished washing Cord's cuts and bruises.

"Thank you," Cord said.

"Would you like some food?" Juan said. "I can't release your hands, but you can eat off a plate."

"I would," Cord said. "Before you get the food, could you roll me a smoke first?"

Juan dug out Cord's pouch and paper and fixed a cigarette. He placed it between Cord's lips and struck a match.

"Obliged," Cord said.

"I'll be back with food," Juan said.

"Could you leave the door open?" Cord said. "It stinks in here."

# FIFTY-THREE

James stepped out onto the porch with the Winchester rifle at the ready when he heard a rider arrive outside the house.

The sky was darkening and James couldn't see the man's face.

"Stay where you are or I'll shoot you in the saddle," James said.

"No need for that," Teasel said. "I'm Mr. Parker's foreman. I have a message."

"What is your message?" James said.

"Mr. Parker thinks things have gone far enough," Teasel said. "He wants to meet with you and talk things over. He'll be at the saloon midnight tonight waiting on you."

James nodded. "All right, you gave me his message. Now get off my property."

Teasel backed his horse up, turned and rode away.

"What's this called?" Cord said as he took a bite of the sweet cake Juan gave him. Cord had to use two hands to eat the cake as they were still roped together tightly.

"It is cake made with carrots," Juan said.

"Carrots?" Cord said. "Tasty."

"I will leave you a cup of coffee," Juan said.

"Thank you."

Juan left the door open and lit a lantern hanging on the wall on the way out. Cord finished the cake and was awkwardly sipping coffee with two hands when Teasel walked into the root cellar.

"Stand up," Teasel said.

Cord slowly managed to get to his feet.

"Johansen is walking into a stacked deck tonight," Teasel said. "I rode out to Johansen's place and told him Parker wants to meet him at the saloon at midnight to talk things over. A gunfighter named Jack Shea will be there to do the talking for Parker. Know him?"

"Only by reputation," Cord said.

Teasel pulled the knife from his gun belt and cut through the ropes on Cord's wrist to free his hands.

"You got three hours to stop Johansen from getting killed," Teasel said. "I figure if you ride hard, you can catch him on the road. Your horse is saddled, and your guns are slung over it."

"Why the change of heart?" Cord said.

"I'm no murderer," Teasel said. "I got to thinking on the way here from Johansen's. I got greedy and I have to live with my sins, but I'm no murderer. Let me get those irons off your legs."

Teasel dug a key out of his pocket, knelt down and removed the shackles and then stood up.

"Sorry about putting the boots to you," Teasel said. "I'm clearing out tonight. I've had enough of Parker and his ranch."

Cord extended his right hand.

Teasel looked at it and then slowly took it, and the two men shook.

"Better ride hard," Teasel said.

Sarah sat in the chair on the porch and waited for James to come out so she could talk some sense into him.

Instead a sleepy-eyed Seth in bare feet opened the door and walked out.

"Ma, what's going on?" Seth said. "Why is Pa getting dressed?"

"Go inside, Seth," Sarah said. "Go back to bed."

"But, Ma."

"Seth, please do as I ask," Sarah said.

James stepped out fully dressed and wearing a jacket to conceal the heavy Colt revolver in his belt.

"Listen to your mother, son," James said.

Sarah stood up.

"You're not seriously going to meet Parker," Sarah said.

"I have to," James said. "This has gone far enough. If he's willing to talk, the least I can do is listen to what he has to say."

James stepped off the porch.

Sarah followed him as he walked to the corral.

"Parker didn't ask you there to talk," Sarah said. "He plans to kill you, James. Don't you see that?"

"In town? In front of witnesses?" James said as he opened the corral gate.

"He owns the town and everybody in it," Sarah said.

"Not everybody," James said.

"James, listen to me," Sarah said. "Let's get away from here right now. I hate this place. It's nothing but work. There isn't even a church or school for Seth."

"Don't say that," James said. "You love this place as much as I do."

"He'll kill you, James," Sarah said. "His men will shoot you down, and you know it. Think of our new son. I can't raise him alone. Please listen to me, James. Please."

James led the team out to the wagon.

"My mind is made up, honey," he said. "Now don't count me out before I even get there. Besides, Parker has nothing to gain by killing me."

Sarah started to cry and fell to her knees.

James started to hitch the team to the wagon.

Sarah composed herself, stood up, walked to the woodpile and picked up a heavy log. She carried the log like a club to the wagon.

"James?" she said.

He turned around and when he did Sarah swung the heavy log and smashed James in his injured ribs with all her weight behind the blow.

James fell to his knees, looked at Sarah and collapsed in a heap on the ground.

Seth ran off the porch.

"Ma, you hit Pa with a log," Seth said.

Sarah tossed the log aside.

"It was the only way to stop him," she said. "Help me get him inside."

Sarah and Seth gently took hold of James by the shoulders and lifted him to a seated position. Half conscious, James moaned softly.

The sound of a horse riding hard froze them in place.

Sarah reached for the Colt tucked into James's belt and cocked it.

"Ma," Seth said.

"Quiet," Sarah said.

The horse and rider appeared. It was too dark to see a face, but then the rider gracefully slid from the saddle and walked to them.

"I came here to stop him, but I see you beat me to it," Cord said.

"He was going to meet Parker in town," Sarah said.

"I know," Cord said. He knelt for a moment to look at James. "I guess no one can fault him not showing up. Need a hand getting him inside?"

Sarah looked into Cord's eyes. The words on her tongue

wouldn't come out and she shook her head no.

"Storm's coming," Cord said. "Best get him inside."

Cord walked to his horse.

"Wait," Sarah said.

Cord turned and looked at her. They held eye contact for a few seconds.

"I know," Cord said and mounted up.

A moment later he rode away into the darkness.

"Mr. Cord knows what, Ma?" Seth said.

"That we are grateful to him," Sarah said. "Let's get your father inside."

"Pa's coming around," Seth said.

"He'll be all right, Seth," Sarah said. "Now lift."

The thickening storm clouds covered the moon, and Cord rode the last mile into town in near total darkness. Lightning started to flash. When he reached the edge of town, the rain began to fall.

A few faint lights glowed in windows of a few buildings as he rode down Main Street to the saloon.

The sheriff's office was dark, locked up tight.

The doors to the saloon were shut. Lanterns were lit inside.

Cord dismounted and tied the reins to the post on the street.

As he reached for the doors and opened them, lightning flashed, quickly followed by a loud booming clap of thunder.

Cord entered the saloon and closed the doors behind him.

To his right Jack Shea sat at a table some forty feet away. He was drinking coffee and smoking a cigarette.

Past Shea, Parker sat with a cigar and a glass of brandy.

The only other person in the saloon was a frightened-looking bartender behind the bar.

Cord walked directly to the bar.

"Rye whiskey," Cord said.

The bartender looked at Cord and then shifted his eyes to look at Parker.

"I'm over here," Cord said.

The bartender set a glass on the bar with a shaky hand and then grabbed a bottle of rye whiskey, but his hand shook so badly, he couldn't pour.

"I'll do it," Cord said and took the bottle and filled his shot glass.

Holding the shot glass, Cord turned and looked directly at Jack Shea.

"You must be Jack Shea," Cord said as he took a small sip.

Shea grinned. "And you must be Cord."

"I wouldn't aggravate Shea if I was you, Cord," Parker said.

Cord looked at Parker. "You wanted to settle this. That's what I'm here for," he said.

"With Johansen," Parker said. "I'll settle with you another time."

"Why wait? I'm here," Cord said.

"Another time, Cord," Parker said. "I'm waiting for Johansen."

"He isn't coming," Cord said. "He's laid up with busted ribs."

"Too bad," Parker said. "I guess I'll have to reschedule."

Cord looked at Shea.

"What do you say, Shea?" Cord said.

"I told you not to aggravate Shea, Cord," Parker said.

"I say that you're a yellow-belly Yankee lover," Shea said.

Cord tossed back his rye and set the glass on the bar.

Behind Cord the bartender walked to the far end of the bar.

"And I say you're a backstabbing, no-good coward," Cord said.

Shea grinned as he stood up and walked away from the table.

"Can you back those words?" Shea said.

"Can you?" Cord said.

Cord and Shea stared at each other for many long and silent seconds.

Shea made his move first. His right hand was lightning fast as he drew his Colt, cocked it and fired.

Cord was a fraction of a second faster.

The difference between life and death.

Cord's first shot struck Shea high in the left side of his chest.

Shea's shot nicked Cord in the left shoulder.

As Cord's bullet tore a hole in Shea's lung, he fell against a table and it broke under his weight.

Cord waited for Shea to slowly grind his way to his feet. Blood poured from the hole in his chest.

"You're good, Cord," Shea said. "Real good."

Cord cocked his .44, aimed and shot Shea in the heart.

"Better than you'll ever be," Cord said.

After Shea hit the floor there was a moment of silence.

Cord heard Parker move and turned to his left.

Parker was on his feet with a cocked revolver in his hand.

"You killed my son, you miserable son of a bitch!" Parker screamed and pulled the trigger.

Cord fanned his .44 and shot Parker three times.

Parker hit the floor, dead on impact.

Cord slowly replaced his Colt into the holster and said, "Bartender, I'll have another shot of rye."

When Cord's request went unanswered, he turned to find the bartender wasn't there. He looked over the bar. The bartender was dead on the floor, killed by Parker's stray bullet.

Cord filled his shot glass and tossed back the shot.

"Drinks are on the house," he said.

# FIFTY-FOUR

James was in terrible pain, so Sarah fixed a packet of the morphine-laced sleeping powder Tobey gave her and fed it to him.

Inside of ten minutes James was sound asleep.

The lightning and thunder had subsided, and the rain was now a steady pelt against the roof. The house was damp. Sarah tossed a few logs into the fireplace and got a fire going.

At the pump she filled the teapot with water and set it on the stove.

That's when she heard a horse outside the front door.

She went to the window to look out. The lantern was still lit on the porch, and she saw Cord standing beside his horse at the bottom of the steps.

Sarah closed her eyes. Oh, good God, dear God, I am asking you for the strength, she thought.

She went out to the porch and closed the door.

Cord stared at her.

She was in her bare feet, and the rainwater was cold on her skin.

"I've come for you," Cord said.

Sarah looked at the first step on the porch. She knew that if she took the first she would take the rest and never come back.

"I know," she said softly.

Sarah's left foot inched toward the first step.

She held the pose for many long seconds.

Then she pulled her foot back.

"But you can't go?" Cord said.

"No."

Cord looked at her for a few more seconds, then mounted his horse, touched his hat to Sarah and quietly rode away into the rain.

As he reached the road, Sarah's foot hit the first step and then the second, and then Cord was gone and she stood there in the rain and started to cry.

# 1930

By 1890 Wyoming was a state. Parker was long forgotten, and in another ten years Brooks was just another deserted ghost town littering the old west. Its history and the range war died along with its people.

I got permission from the Wyoming Film Commission to use Brooks to film my movie there. The set decorators took six weeks to rebuild the town. They did a good job, right down to the brass doorknobs on the hotel.

I was reading script notes in a chair at the hotel. Actors in costume rehearsed on the streets while set decorators added some finishing touches.

Then a gleaming Cadillac came riding down Main Street. I jumped up from the chair and was filled with a sudden excitement.

I raced down to meet my brother's car.

It stopped and the passenger door opened.

Cord was still tall and fit. His hair was silver, as was his beard. It took many years to find him, but it was well worth it to me. I heard that after he left my mother on the steps of our old farmhouse, he took the two hundred and fifty head of cattle owed to him by Parker and drove them to his ranch in California.

In 1910 he took advantage of land he purchased in the Napa Valley and switched over to wine making. That's how I located him. The private detective I hired found Cord through his wines

266

sold in a thousand stores.

He never married.

When my father died in 1915, my mother told me this story. It's the basis for the script that's taken me fifteen years to write. She never told my father that my brother was actually Cord's son or that Cord's first name was Jesse. When I told her I was filming the story as the first-ever talking western, she begged me for a part as an extra.

How could I refuse?

Ma would play Mrs. Cullen, owner of the boarding house that she stayed in the night I had my appendix removed.

"Mr. Cord, this is the writer and director of the film, my brother Seth," my brother said.

Cord looked at me carefully.

"Did you rebuild this entire town for this movie?" Cord said.

"And my farmhouse," I said.

"Your brother tells me you want me to be something called a technical advisor," Cord said.

"Yes. To correct any mistakes made on how things were really done back in the old west," I said.

Cord looked at the actors rehearsing on the street. One of them was wearing a jacket with tassels and had a gleaming six-gun in a polished holster.

"For one thing we didn't dress like rodeo clowns," Cord said.

I nodded. "I'd like you to read the script later," I said. "But right now there is a woman who would like to see you. She's an extra in the movie. She's in the hotel lobby behind me. She said she has an old horse brush that belongs to you."

"Wait," Cord said. "You said farmhouse. The Johansen farm?"

"I'm Seth Johansen," I said.

Cord stared at me. His eyes were every bit as powerful as they were forty-eight years ago when I was a little boy.

"One thing you should know about my mother is she really

hates to be kept waiting," I said.

Cord looked up at the hotel door. Then he walked past me as if I weren't there and took the steps two at a time, opened the door and went inside.

Jesse came and stood beside me.

"Think Ma will tell him he's my father?" Jesse said.

"I think he's already figured that out," I said. "Come on; let's go get some real clothes for the actors."

# ABOUT THE AUTHOR

**Ethan J. Wolfe** is a native of New York City. He has traveled and studied the American West extensively. He is the author of the western novels *The Last Ride, The Regulator* and *The Range War of '82*. He is presently working on the second novel in the Regulator series.